PENNY FROM HEAVEN

Charlie Parkes

Copyright © 2023 Charlie Parkes

All rights reserved

The characters, locations and events portrayed in this book are fictitious. Any similarity to real persons, living or dead, is coincidental and not intended by the author.

No part of this book may be reproduced, or stored in a retrieval system, or transmitted in any form or by any means, electronic, mechanical, photocopying, recording, or otherwise, without express written permission of the publisher.

ISBN: 9798870584904

Cover design by: Author

Elizabeth –My soulmate

I hope my words will live on,
After I am gone.

                                                                  AUTHOR

CONTENTS

Title Page
Copyright
Dedication
Epigraph
Prologue
The Road North   1
Wild Camping   10
Inverie   17
Heaven's Gateway   38
Meeting the Locals   69
Soul Searching and Sea Trout   81
Kilt and Haggis   91
Lobster and Crab   100
Landy and the Mermaid's Pool   122
Pandora's box?   135
Glorious Twelfth   140
Rob and the Leviathan   147
Dear Roland!   153
Rabbit and Spar'rib Pie   164
Hollywood comes to town   169
Wiltshire   182

The Premiere	194
Book Ends	199
Acknowledgement	209
About The Author	215
Books By This Author	219

PROLOGUE

Dear Gentle Reader,

What you are about to read is drawn from my own memories, life experiences and imagination.

It is early May as I set out on my pilgrimage. I am the narrator of the tale, and a character in it. The other main characters are Penny, her brother Roland, the friends I make in a remote Scottish enclave, and Anja my car.

You will encounter many facts, people and locations, but is it a tale of fiction and fantasy or one of truth and substance?

You will need to read to the end to find out.

No Peeking!

THE ROAD NORTH

The Angel of the North is one of the most viewed pieces of art in the world, seen by more than one person every second, that is 90,000 every day or 33 million every year. That is why it fills me with dread whenever I plan a route or drive past it. Why? Because all those viewers are in vehicles on the A1 and if the Angel is in Heaven then for me the road is a descent into motorway hell as it sweeps sluggishly downhill and around Gateshead. I am conscious of complying with the speed limit while avoiding overtakers and undertakers pushing and shoving their way through. I do not know why it annoys me so much, but it does, and I try to avoid it at all costs.

Angel of the North

Legends in the Bible state the entrance to hell is in a valley near Jerusalem, one of three on Earth; one under the sea, and a third in the desert. If the Bible were re-written today, it would identify a fourth on the A1 road works below the Angel of the

North. On a good day, my stress is short-lived as I start the rise from Satan's lair up a long gradient to my view of heaven, the wide-open spaces of Northumberland, vast areas of heather moorland, rolling hills, sun glinting on the distant sea and the occasional glimpse of golden sand. Unless, it is raining of course! However, Northumberland is only the foothills to my heaven, as my journey will take me through the Scottish Borders, moving ever North West until I reach the sea to begin a new life, a new adventure, a life of peace and solitude.

Before I get to my ultimate destination, I have four visits to make to my two sisters at Thropton, near Rothbury and Tweedbank, near Melrose, then onwards to Dalmally on the River Orchy to see an old friend; finally, a pilgrimage to Inverie on the Knoydart peninsula. But more of that later. Both sisters think I am mad when I explain my venture to them, especially at my age, and in my overweight, unfit, unhealthy condition. Although my new physiotherapist has done a great job, straightening my spine and reducing that nagging relentless ache across my pelvis. His surgery walls hung with glorious pictures of golden deserted beaches and heather-clad mountains may have provided the final trigger to escape urban life. It is what I have wanted to do many times and if I leave it any longer, death or total infirmity will overcome me like many of my peers and friends.

I suppose Scotland was instilled in me in the 1960's when my parents embarked upon three-week caravan holidays outside normal school holidays. Such absences were not subject to fines in those days, but on my return, the kids were surprised to see me, thinking I had moved schools. I have no idea if it affected my education. I doubt it. I studiously did my homework and tried hard but as the reports said, "Could do better." I think I was just reluctant to revise what I found to be boring, and my eyes would glaze over and the pages blur in front of me. I did exit the sixth form after the first year when my father changed jobs and we moved away, so it was time to taste the world of work, leave home, go into digs or lodgings and start to learn about life.

After forty-seven years as a police cadet, a constable rising to chief inspector then a civilian or police staff employee investigating complaints and corruption, I came to think I had learnt more than enough about life and man's inhumanity to man. My education was complete. It was time for me to do something I wanted to do and this was the start of that journey. My career and family life had periods of stress when I could not see a way out or forward, and I longed to run away and live in seclusion in a cottage on a Scottish shore. Responsibilities to family and the need to pay the mortgage and day-to-day living costs, soon put paid to such daydreams until the summer of 2023.

For years, we have had warnings of the impact of climate change, but now the dangers were becoming increasingly obvious. In Antarctica, Emperor penguin chicks drowned as ice broke up early due to sea warming. Temperatures soared across mainland Europe with wildfires engulfing thousands of acres of forest, driving residents and holidaymakers to seek refuge on the beaches and in the sea. Across the world, floods, landslides and hurricanes filled the daily news.

In the UK, we are witnessing subtle changes through higher temperatures as species of all kinds migrate from the hotter warmer regions to take up residence in our cooler climes. Farmers are planning for crops that will survive in warmer, drier, weather. In effect, everything is moving northwards and in a relatively short time, we may find Costa del Skegness or Scarborough de Compostela replacing the Mediterranean hotspots.

2023 saw the first anniversary of the Russian "special military operation" against Ukraine and the western powers, fuelling fears of atomic warfare and the opportunity for humankind to destroy life on earth with a global nuclear retaliation. Thinking ahead, perhaps fifty years, I know I will not be around, but how will my grandchildren cope with climate change and survive nuclear holocaust? What could I do to safeguard their future? Could I buy a dwelling or a plot of land in such isolation that it would offer a chance of survival?

Occasionally, I had briefly considered finding a bolthole where we could survive. I think the idea came from a shooting and fishing holiday trip to Tomatin on the River Findhorn. Sixteen of us took the Kyllachy estate for a week self catering in Kyllachy House, a large comfortable Victorian sporting lodge built in 1886 for William MacKintosh, Lord Kyllachy, a distinguished judge. It is set above the Findhorn River and surrounded by majestic moorland. One couple from Norway had bought a plot of land with a cabin and lived there in total isolation for long periods. It was their bolthole if their world turned upside down.

Kyllaky House

Holidays with the family are always periods when I tend to think about life and ideas for a new book. Being hard of hearing, I am often oblivious to their conversations and my brain is free to run riot, delving into its databanks and throwing up ideas and memories. This was a special holiday to celebrate our fifty years of marriage and granddaughter Charlotte's 14th birthday. A large coastal property accommodated my wife, Elizabeth, daughter Kathryn and Dean her partner, the grandchildren William and Charlotte and son Christopher and husband Karl and two dogs, Millie a brown Labrador and Theo "The Mexican" Chihuahua.

The Anchorage is a stunning contemporary house with breathtaking views across the salt marshes out to sea. The "upside-down" design allowed Liz and I to lay in bed, open the patio doors and look out on uninterrupted views across the marsh to the sea and the big Norfolk skies, occasionally waving to passers-by. The rental property was located opposite a short lane across the marshland to a pebble beach constantly occupied by all manner of campers. Not just mobile caravans but four different DIY van conversions; a young couple in a small van had a mattress on a platform in the back, an older couple had a slightly larger van, a Ford Transit, and appeared to have two narrow claustrophobic double-decker bunks. Two single men appeared to have made living space in their work vans, and I later saw one of them in a nearby village working at a building site. A father and son were probably bonding in a new Landrover Defender for a couple of nights. I began investigating wild camping in my daydream to live in the back of my Skoda SUV, drawing up lists of equipment and even trying to squeeze my long body into the car as a trial run. I browsed awnings attached to the back with the rear door open allowing my long legs to dangle outwith the vehicle.

Beach Road Salthouse, Norfolk

All that data from earlier daydreams came flooding back. But, where would be the safest place in a nuclear holocaust? Wikipedia identified the potential nuclear targets if our world leaders pressed the button. It is not difficult to guess that London, the Royal family, ports and airports, and most of southern England would be first in direct line, followed by a rolling barrage of cities and strategic bases as far as Glasgow and Edinburgh, Aberdeen and the North Sea oilfields. The obvious choice for a bunker or bolthole would be the far northwest of Scotland, midges or no midges.

We know from history that the Second World War ended with two small Hydrogen bombs, small by today's standard that is. Since then the world has lived in relative safety in the belief that no world leader would be stupid enough to set the end of the planet in motion. Instead a Cold War existed between the WW2 allies, United States and the Soviet Union, East v West in an ideological and geopolitical struggle for global influence by the two superpowers.

Atomic Bombs Hiroshima and Nagasaki

The nuclear arms race was a competition for supremacy in nuclear warfare between the United States, the Soviet Union, and their respective allies to create the largest and most powerful nuclear stockpiles. Minor states sought to develop their own atomic weapons to safeguard their own countries, just like North Korea.

Aside from the nuclear arms race, the struggle for dominance is conducted now via indirect means, such as psychological warfare, propaganda campaigns, espionage, far-reaching embargoes, sports diplomacy, and technological competitions like the Space Race.

In my childhood we were recovering from the deprivations of WW2. Rationing finally ceased in the fifties and we all saw a brighter future, confident that we had survived another war to end all wars. All was well until October 1962 when the Soviet Union installed missiles on the island of Cuba, ninety miles from Florida, in response to American deployments in Italy and Turkey. The confrontation is widely considered the closest the Cold War came to escalating into full-scale nuclear war. President John F. Kennedy imposed a naval quarantine around Cuba and then negotiated with Soviet First Secretary, Nikita Khrushchev. Removing missiles from Cuba and Turkey restored confidence in a lasting peace and a secure future.

Our secret weapon was James Bond, our answer to Superman, who was able to foil and destroy any megalomaniac with little more than a Walther PPK pistol, Q's gadgetry and a car equipped with machine guns and an ejector seat. We had no need to worry. We were more concerned about buying our own house, fitted carpet, avocado coloured bathroom suites and colour television. There were plans in the event of a nuclear attack on the UK but they were hopelessly inadequate to deal with the impact and aftermath of a strike. We were still operating at WW2 levels of response and had no comprehension of the death and devastation, breakdown in structures, communications, radiation, food and water supplies. I fear it would be little different today.

The Wikipedia entry on the Cuban missile crisis describes Operation Candid, a plan to spirit the Royal Family away to isolated country houses in Scotland, not Balmoral but secluded sporting lodges, and the plan had contingencies for different situations depending on the political situation and the amount of preparation time. Queen Elizabeth and Prince Phillip would disperse to country houses away from London and evacuate to sea on the royal yacht, HMY Britannia, a floating bunker hidden in the lochs of northwest Scotland. Moving at night, Britannia would sail from one loch to another, shielded from Soviet radar by the mountains.

Royal Yacht Britannia

If north-west Scotland was the safest bet for Her Majesty then it was good enough for me, so using satellite images on Google, I scanned the north-west Scottish coastline for an isolated sea loch or inlet, where I would start my search for a suitable property. A cottage or croft next to or near the sea, a water supply, woodland for fuel, habitat for game, deer, rabbits for food, perhaps some reasonable soil for growing subsistence crops, grazing for livestock and a freshwater loch to fish. A tall order indeed.

WILD CAMPING

I transformed my SUV, a Skoda Kodiaq, nicknamed Anja to reflect her Slovakian roots, into a bed on wheels. Bijou, but enough space for one person to exist, with the occasional night of luxury in a remote B&B. We do take a lot for granted when packing our daily needs into a car, toilet tissue to matches, fuel for a stove, washing line for your smalls, soap, detergent, clothes, shaving gear, and so on. We cram our essentials into a couple of cases for a holiday flight but on this trip I needed to travel light, but still have everything I might need to feed and support myself.

I scheduled the 1st of May 2024 for lift off, hoping that the weather would be mild and early enough in the season to avoid the midges, but I still carried a midge hat and plenty of deterrent. I had not attempted to sell my ideas to the family; Granddad was off on a personal solo mission to visit Inverie on the Knoydart Peninsula and would be gone for a couple of weeks. 0700 on the 1st May, Anja and I set off at a steady gallop, no need to try and outrace all the lorries and vans on the M1 north. We both seemed to be happy with our progress especially north of the A64 Leeds to York road where the A1 is quieter.

Next waypoint was the appropriately named Scotch Corner and five miles along the A66 we turned on to a country lane to a Stoneygate Farm Cafe at Ravensworth. Liz and I have travelled the A66 many times finding regular stopping off points. Stoneygate was a recent and most welcome find just off the A66, but well away from the masses cramming into the hotspots. I would normally have had a bacon or sausage roll but given the need to think well ahead about food provision, self catering etc I decided on a full English breakfast to see me through the day, or longer if need be.

The A66 is a most scenic cross-Pennine road, which, in part, follows the course of the Roman road from Scotch Corner to Penrith. It can be high, wild and windswept with barriers closing it off in severe weather. At other times, like today, the sun shone and the sky blue and clear as we passed the highest point at Stainmore summit of 1,450 feet (440 m) descending towards Brough and onwards to Penrith. I gave Anja a rest in Sainsbury's car park at Penrith and walked over to the John Norris shop. Over the years, I have been a regular customer when travelling north to fish for salmon, an opportunity to stock up with new flies, waders, clothing and rods. Back home it was also my first port of call to shop online. Today I was stocking up with basic sea and freshwater angling supplies, spinning and sea fishing lures, monofilament line, worming hooks, and some wee double trout flies for the rivers and wild, un-fished lochs. I recognised the man serving in the tackle department, a retired police officer. I asked if the flies are guaranteed to catch fish. I knew his response, "Oh aye, There's a guarantee stamped underneath the barb!"

There is also an excellent artisan bakery on the Market Square so I called at JJ Grahams to stock up on fresh bread, scones, pie and honey glazed ham. Anja was waiting for me, cooled after her rest and ready to head for the Scottish Borders. I mentioned earlier my dislike of the A1 at Gateshead but my younger sister had recently moved to the lovely village of Thropton, near Rothbury, and the A66 is way off track. However, my plan was to visit my elder sister at Melrose taking her out for the day, and have a sibling reunion with Jane.

At Gretna Green, I veered sharp right to Langholm, Hawick and finally Melrose. Pat knew I was only stopping a couple of days, the bed was ready and we tucked into my goodies from Grahams. Again, I hid the full truth about my pilgrimage, explaining I wanted to fulfil a dream of wild camping even if I ended up in a

B&B or hotel. Being an intrepid traveller to the Galapagos Isles, New Zealand and Bermuda she understood my mission. Jane also had a wanderlust yearning for Mull and moved from the Midlands to her idyllic bungalow adjacent to the Northumbrian coast.

4th May and Anja purred away via a diesel stop at Asda in Galashiels. It is sound advice to top up whenever and wherever you can as you go into the far North West. The scenic A68 took us northwards towards Edinburgh, the last major conurbation in our way and if traffic allowed, we would progress steadily west on the ring road. I recall the first time I passed here after the new Forth Road Bridge opened, marvelling at its huge glistening slender sails, like three gossamer winged butterflies.

Firth of Forth Bridges

I also recalled travelling the opposite direction and being taken aback by two giant horses' heads hovering over the mature trees on the opposite side of the motorway. The Kelpies were unknown to me at that time, but a trompe-l'oeil effect tricked my brain into thinking the heads turned to watch my progress as I passed.

The Kelpies

The motorway roughly tracked the Firth of Forth crossing the River Forth near its junction with River Teith and heading North West. Callendar will be forever enshrined in my mind as the fictional Scottish town of Tannochbrae, the home of Dr Finlay a general medical practice TV drama set in the late 1920s and broadcast in the early sixties. Just time for a stroll a pot of Earl Grey and piece of shortbread. Quite correctly, Anja had veered off the M9 outside Dunblane and we were now on A and B roads but far less traffic. For me this was the start of Scotland, The Trossachs, a picturesque area of wooded glens, braes, and lochs lying to the east of Loch Lomond, representing a microcosm of a typical highland landscape.

Scotland has some uniquely beautiful romantic place names and as I pass Falls of Leny, Lochearnhead, Balquidder and Crianlarich I think of The Proclaimers song, Letter from America:

When you go will you send back a letter from America?

Take a look up the rail track from Miami to Canada

Lochaber no more,

> Sutherland no more
>
> Lewis no more,
>
> Skye no more

Would I be singing this song on my return? Would I return?

Anja pressed on along the A84 and A85 clinging to the shore of Loch Lubnaig on her port side, Balquidder and Lochearnhead. A short breather to view the Glen Ogle viaduct that is worth a photo but nowhere near as spectacular as Glenfinnan, and no longer in use other than a foot and cycle path. At the top of Glen Ogle, Anja bears west into Glen Dochart to Crianlarich and Tyndrum where I can take the low road to my intended destination Dalmally, or the longer and more picturesque high road to Bridge of Orchy following the River Orchy down the glen of the same name. The river is narrow descending through rocky clefts and tree-lined pools before opening out in to magnificent fly-fishing water with long stretches of streamy pools. I explain to Anja that the picture below is her predecessor, Betsy the Freelander, on the Orchy.

River Orchy

I stop at Black Duncan reminiscing to Anja that I caught my

first salmon in this pool, a tale that features in my book of Shaggy Dog Stories. At Dalmally, we climb the long curling drive to a bungalow high on the bank side above the river. A warm welcome was expected and received from my fishing friend Steve, now the proud owner of the bungalow and several miles of prime water on the Orchy. It was his retirement present having sold his business but was now just as busy maintaining the banks and all the associated work connected with river management.

Steve made his break from the monotony of work to enjoy the fruits of his new labours. A confirmed bachelor he lived alone apart from fishing pals and female companions, so was keen to have company and swap gossip from home. I spent three nights with him, dining at the local hotel or the chippy. A cooked breakfast was compulsory and in the evening perhaps salmon or venison with whatever vegetables, we could acquire locally. I recall on my first visit in the mid eighties that the local shop stocked little more than turnips and potatoes. When asked about something more exotic like carrots the shopkeeper stated he had only just go the locals onto cabbage. A salutary lesson here on advance planning for provisions and fuel.

Steve was an inveterate smoker, always giving up and always failing. If the shop was shut it meant a visit to the hotel to buy ciggies at the bar. It catered for the "Coach tripping bedwetters" as Steve called them, old people just like we are now. It cannot be said that we were miles from civilisation although Steve did say, "Anywhere is a hundred miles from here." Not strictly true as Oban, a major port and gateway to the isles, is only 24 miles but seems a lot further on the twisting undulating A85.

My next destination was in fact Fort William a mere fifty odd miles from Dalmally, but I wanted to revisit my childhood caravan holidays pitched at Ganavan Sands near Oban, where I could wander at will to my heart's content. Father and I played on the challenging pitch and putt course and one evening we saw a small fishing boat enter the bay laying a net in a circle and scooping up the sea trout. Acting on information received, we walked the coastline to find the sea trout, which we did one very hot and sunny afternoon. We could see the fish, but knew not how to catch them, so I was most surprised when father stripped naked and dived in after them. Like father like son. The following day a trip to Oban bought him a sea trout from the quay.

Ganavan Sands, Oban

INVERIE

Fort William commands the top of Loch Linnhe bringing back memories of my wife's 50th birthday on a rail weekend trip culminating with a trip on the Jacobite West Highland Line, now known worldwide as Hogwarts Express. It was a remarkable trip and experience steaming out of Fort William in the mist and rain and crossing the viaduct in the sun at Glenfinnan station. It was here in 1745 that Bonnie Prince Charlie arrived at the head of Loch Shiel to gather the clans for his march on London and claim the English crown. He reached Derby before turning back and so it was always a treat to go with my grandfather on the trolley bus to view the Bonnie Prince's room in the museum. A magnificent statute of him on horseback commemorates the event.

Bonnie Prince Charlie, Derby

Gentle reader I digress. I can only apologise for my brain that insists on digging up these memories. The sun again gave way to mist and rain as we climbed over Glencoe traversing the spectacular but desolate and unwelcoming Rannoch Moor.

Corrour Halt, West Highland Line

At Corrour Halt, I saw a young woman leave the train and walk off into the mist, sparking an idea for my first novel, The Hidden Glen. Emma, my heroine sets off from Glenfinnan on a three-day trek staying in bothies, but is overcome by a violent storm only to be rescued by her Prince Charming. She recovers in the hidden glen, continuing her journey to Inverie on the peninsula of Knoydart, across the sea from Skye and just north of Mallaig. Knoydart can only be accessed on foot or by boat so my diversion from my expedition was to visit Inverie and the locations I used in the novel.

Like Emma, I chose to stay in a B&B so that I would be clean, fresh and ready for the ferry, but first I had to make my way to Mallaig. From Fort William, one can again take the low road or the high road. The A830 is the shortest and most direct route, especially now that the road has been straightened from the time of my youth, where we stopped to walk barefoot on the whistling sands. A most picturesque route, but I had all day and retraced my past steps over the Corran ferry and the loch side road to Strontian and Acharacle located at the opposite end of Loch Shiel.

It was now lunchtime and luckily the community cafe was in full swing. A chalkboard sign invited passers-by to call for soup and sandwiches. If I said "No" I would remain isolated in my car and hungry so I said "Yes", most definitely yes! Volunteers provided a choice of four soups, bacon or sausage sandwiches and a buffet of homemade cakes. Pay as much as you want or can afford. I sat alone with my feast but not for long, as an elderly resident pulled up a chair for a chat. Her relatives lived in Derbyshire and she had been to Matlock etc etc. She left me to continue with my meal but my host, the man serving the soup, a retired dentist who had fled the rat race to sail his yacht around the islands, took her seat. He had achieved what I was seeking.

River Shiel

I walked my substantial lunch down with a stroll by River Shiel, a most fishy river and imagined myself in a tussle with a fresh run salmon. Anja burbled along happily at a steady space through miles of open isolated country on a single narrow road, finally reaching the coast at Glenuig and joining the Fort William road at Lochailort for the final push to Mallaig. Calling at the ferry terminal, I checked its location, parking and my booking for the foot ferry. A quick stroll around the small town and harbour, a pot of tea, and watching The Jacobite steam into Mallaig station.

The Jacobite, Mallaig Station

Retracing my steps, I stopped on the banks of the River Morar where it exits Loch Morar to the sea, a short but most glorious ribbon of aqua blue bounded by pure white soft sand. I needed somewhere to start my wild camping in earnest on return from Inverie the following day, after a final taste of civilised luxury at a B&B. My excuse was that I did not have time to experiment with packing the car and getting to the ferry on time. The typical modern white-painted bungalow with slate roof overlooked the estuary and I spent the evening walking the shore and contemplating the start of my expedition in earnest.

River Morar

A full hearty Scottish breakfast with haggis instead of black pudding and Anja took me to the ferry. In years past, I had crossed on the car ferry from Skye to Mallaig looking longingly to see Inverie through the mist. This time I would approach in clear bright sun to land on the small harbour. I sat by the slipway for a while getting my bearings and looking south to the summit of A Chruach standing guard over the bay, its steep sides descending from 395m to sea level by the shore. A Chruach and the harbour feature strongly in the novel with A Chruach being one of the gateways to the Hidden Glen and the point where Emma returned to reality.

A Chruach Inverie – Gateway to The Hidden Glen

In my backpack, I had several copies of The Hidden Glen, one for the host of the B&B where Emma stayed, one for the landlord at the Forge Inn and one for Mrs Mackay who worked at the Community Shop. As I sat contemplating the scene, I reasoned how to explain that I had not been brave enough to use my real name as author of The Hidden Glen and choosing Carla as my pen name. I could not imagine a young female readership buying a romantic novel written by a crusty old bloke! Perhaps I should have followed E.L.James example in Fifty Shades of Grey. I am often asked if there is any "you know what" in the novel but my response is always "about half a shade of grey."

My first visit was The Gathering, a renowned B&B and restaurant run by Cara Gray, its reviews just as impressive now as when I located Emma there. I have found that playing the part of a "lost old gentleman" attracts some sympathy and so I explained my expedition, walkabout, pilgrimage, call it what you will. I proffered a free copy, which was received tentatively as Cara thumbed the pages, smiled and invited me for a coffee. Gratefully received and the ice broken. I had quoted her in the book when in conversation with Emma and apologised for taking her words in vain. I think she was quite amused and delighted and wished me well as I parted for The Forge.

The Old Forge Inverie

It was time for lunch at The Forge and I continued my old gentleman routine with the landlord, as I explained it was here that Emma met Dougie the local stalker who knew of the Hidden Glen but had never found it. The next day Emma revealed the vital information that he had to climb A Chruach and "follow his dream" to find the path into the glen. Dougie was a figment of my imagination as was his lady friend, the widow McKay who worked at the Community Shop. Now was the time for the old gentleman to be a little mischievous. Looking round the goods on display, a young assistant asked if she could help.

"Oh yes please. I was wondering if Mrs McKay still worked here?" She looked puzzled.

"I don't know of a Mrs McKay but I will ask." and disappeared into the backroom. Shortly I was surrounded by a helpful group of ladies seeking further information and I played them along as long as I dare, before revealing she was a character from my novel. The ruse worked well with them laughing at my practical joke and wanting to know more about Mrs McKay and her activities with Dougie. It was all great fun and I left with numerous handshakes, kisses and hugs and a promise to buy copies and put the book on sale.

Community Shop Inverie

I wandered round Inverie glowing at the thought that I had achieved this part of my pilgrimage, enjoying the company of such wonderful people and their hospitality. It was time for the ferry and the start of my wilderness expedition proper. It was time to test my mettle as a wild-camper on the sandy shores of the Morar River. My camping site was vacant so I opened the tailgate and constructed the tailgate awning. I had studiously packed everything neatly and in order so the mallet and pegs came to hand readily. With a groundsheet and a chair it felt like home. One begins to appreciate home, a B&B or a hotel and the ability to just walk in to the convenience of warmth, light, running hot water, shower etc etc and especially a toilet. Number ones are easily resolved for a man by a trip to a nearest bush or a dip in the sea. For number twos one needs a toilet seat fixed to a stool with a heavy-duty doggy bag attached. I soon had that set up ready to go! Toilet tissue and disposable wipes to hand. You quickly appreciate how much we take everyday essentials for granted.

Time for dinner, so out with my Trangia camping stove, a simple methylated spirit burner. Now where did I put those matches? It was simple fare. New potatoes and carrots boiled in the same pan and a couple of excellent sausages from the butcher in Mallaig. Boil the kettle now to wash up and boil it again to brew fresh coffee before settling into my chair with some shortbread to watch the sunset. No telly and no radio so it was an early night ready for an early start.

A pot of Earl Grey started my day after a relatively comfortable night although someone had not turned on the central heating and the annexe was a little chilly. Having boiled water in my miniscule Trangia kettle to wash and wash-up, it was cereals for breakfast with my blood pressure and gout pills. It was time to test the "Number twos" contraption and I found sitting in the middle of my lounge/diner/kitchenette/bedroom to be a rather strange experience. Perhaps in the wilderness I could site it outside and gaze over a sea loch, coffee in hand to enjoy the view. A hole in the ground would replace the giant sized black plastic doggy bag I had to tie up and then find somewhere to dispose of it.

After packing everything away neatly and checking the site was tidy, we were heading east back towards Fort William on the "high road." This was a necessary diversion to circumvent the vast tracts of inaccessible moorland split by long fingers of sea inlets. However, I had one more visit to pay on my Hidden Glen pilgrimage as the road passed Loch nan Uamh in Lochaber and the Prince's Cairn. It was here in July 1745 that the Young Pretender, Bonnie Prince Charlie, first stepped ashore on mainland Great Britain.

Prince's Cairn

Following the failure of the Jacobite rising and a decisive defeat at the Battle of Culloden, Prince Charles Edward Stuart embarked for the Hebrides from Loch nan Uamh in April 1746. Those who have read The Hidden Glen will know that it also marks the entrance to my mystical location. Time for a few photographs and then on to Glenfinnan for a photo stop looking down the glen to view Glenfinnan Monument and the waters of Loch Shiel.

Glennfinan Monument and Loch Shiel

It was time to commence my mission proper to find a bunker to survive a nuclear attack. At Inverary Anja turned west for Applecross. I could have travelled via two ferries onto and off the Isle of Skye but decided the road journey of 100 miles was the best bet given the vagary and timing of ferry services in the Isles. It is a most scenic drive clinging to the coastline, weaving through mountain-lined glens. I was grateful for Anja's flexible low revving diesel engine pulling me quietly up and down the steep inclines and the blessing of an automatic gearbox. All I had to do was to steer and operate the accelerator. Oh and concentrate hard, looking for an escape spot or overtaking point on the single-track roads, but this was nothing compared to what lay ahead, Bealach na Ba, the Pass of the Cattle, an infamous climb into the clouds and descent to the sea.

Described as a twisting mountain pass on the Applecross Peninsula in Wester Ross that is undeniably the most famous section of the North Coast 500 Highland touring route. This single-track road rises over 2,000 feet (0.61 km) and is famous for being one of the most scenic drives in the world, as well as one of the most dangerous due to its tight hairpin bends. I had done the ascent before from the hamlet of Applecross on the coast to reach the viewpoint on top of the world. We started in sunshine but gradually entered misty drizzle in the low cloud. The road is indeed narrow with rocks on the nearside and a long drop on the offside bounded by crash barriers. I was in my trusted Betsy, a Landrover Freelander, narrow with a square bonnet making her very pointable as I edged into the nearside to allow oncoming vehicles to pass. In places, it was only wide enough for a motor cycle to edge past and we exchanged pleasantries as I looked up his nose.

Bealach na Ba – Pass of the cattle

It was a question of looking well ahead for a passing place, and hoping that a mobile home would not loom out of the mist. There is a lot of official advice on taking campervans and caravans over the pass. Certainly not suitable for caravans and for campervans it suggests you do not attempt it unless you can reverse safely. We reached the top with an interesting drive and visibility down to 30 metres! The descent was just as interesting with a staircase of hairpin bends. Towards the bottom, we encountered a large motor-home navigating a hairpin where the road was quite wide and we waited while he shunted back and forth until there was a loud bang as the rear corner collided with the cliff face. However, today was sunny and Anja purred gently on going through her gears to reach the viewpoint. What a view!

Bealach na Ba – Pass of the cattle

Now the descent to the sea; a walk round Applecross, a glance in a couple of touristy shops, the pub, and a walled garden restaurant. A little early for me to eat, but the Garden cafe looked inviting. More inviting was the diesel pump at the filling station before heading northish along the coast and swinging round to Shieldaig, a most pleasant ribbon of white cottages lining the road and public toilets. My return visit to Nanny's cafe was as good as the first with fresh coffee and homemade food for this traveller.

Loch Shieldaig runs into Loch Torridon forming a long inlet to the sea and perhaps an ideal hideout for HMY Britannia. I felt as though from this point on, I would be getting nearer to my ultimate hideout. In this terrain, one has little choice but to follow a single road weaving through the mountains and around the lochs and sea inlets. It was time to find a camp spot for the night and my target was Loch Maree, for which I have a particular affection, having used it as the model for The Hidden Glen and the cover of the book. The Loch is 21.7 km long with a maximum width of four kilometres and is the fourth-largest freshwater loch in Scotland. Within its waters are five large wooded islands and over sixty smaller ones, many of which have their own lochans. Eilean Sùbhainn is the largest island containing a loch also with an island. Like the Hidden Glen, there are remains of a chapel dating to the 8th century. My heroine sails the hidden glen in a small dinghy named bean an locha - Lady of the Loch. How I wish I had a boat now to explore Loch Maree and even camp on its islands. True

isolation in wondrous scenery.

Just beyond the picnic site at Slattadale I found a track off the main road to a grassy spot amid the Caledonian pines overlooking Eilean Ruairidh Mor. As soon as camp was set, I walked to the shore trying to establish where Jerry Sharp took the cover photograph in 2006 and published on Geograph.

Loch Maree

After a long day in the car and a night in the sleeping bag I was in need of some body cleansing so trunks on and I braved a tentative dip in the cold refreshing water. Tiptoeing at first, then creeping slowly into deeper water until I can stand on tiptoe no longer with water lapping round you know where. A deep breath followed by full immersion, then the exultation and rapid strokes in a futile attempt to generate some warmth, but the body became acclimatised, my brain releasing endorphins and for a few minutes was able to swim freely, at one with the environment, generating a sense of freedom never experienced before. Dried and dressed I positively glowed as my Trangia boiled water for my pot of Earl Grey.

Next morning I was keen to set off on the next part of my adventure. Heading West, North and East took me to Poolewe on the sheltered south side of Loch Ewe. The village is little more than a main street of largely white rendered buildings, a hotel and St Maelrubha's Church. It is a stunning location and quite a suitable anchorage for HMY Britannia. Across the bay are Inverewe Gardens, a verdant oasis of foliage and riotously colourful flower collections, contrasting with the wild, heathery crags of the adjoining coasts. These tropical gardens benefit from a warmer microclimate created by the adjacent Gulf Stream. They also attract many visitors and I wanted to avoid tourists as much as possible.

Beyond the Inverewe viewpoint, I was able to turn away from the coast to Loch a' Bhaid-luachraich and hide my camp in the wood. Time for a spot of fishing and sure enough, small, fat yellow-bellied Brown Trout were leaping for large sedge flies in the evening sunset. Finding the right fly to match the hatch is always a problem especially in strange waters but a worm, a wee red brandling is always a good bet, if you can find some. I recall as a lad asking an old Scottish gamekeeper about worms who replied, "Worrums! Worrums! They're scurcer than the fish."

Brandlings love compost heaps or dead branches so turning a few logs over revealed enough bait to entice a fine brace of brownies into my frying pan. I now felt I was in total isolation, no people, no traffic noise, no pollution, a clear star-lit sky. Just the sound of silence pierced by the occasional high-pitched 'kee-yaaa' call of a buzzard or territorial hooting of a Tawny Owl letting me know this was his bit of woodland.

I would not linger long but, felt out of respect, that I should visit the Russian Arctic Convoy Museum at Aultbea remembering those who sailed from the fortified harbour of Loch Ewe to Russia in appalling weather and at the mercy of Nazi U-boats. Aultbea Stores topped up my perishable supplies. I spent a couple of days scouting the area around Mellon Charles, a remote crofting village on the northeast shore of Loch Ewe, but there were no properties for sale and there was nothing to suit my purpose.

It was the end of the road so I retraced my steps to Aultbea and headed for Laide on Gruinard Bay. I was in need of a wash and brush up so a B&B for a couple of nights with a shower and a shave in abundant running hot water made me feel human again. You would expect these B&Bs to be Scots but it seems that many Scots left for the cities or even England. In this case, my hosts were from the Midlands, retired teachers looking for the good life. We had a lot in common and spoke freely after a glass or two of the water of life diluted only with a wee suspicion o'watter. Rob and Mary were interested in my adventure into the wilderness but I kept from them my search for a nuclear hideaway, just in case they thought I was a bit weird. I was interested to hear about the community reaction to Sassenachs invading their Gaelic-speaking enclave. Rob was very clear,

"You cannot survive easily up here without help and support from the community. Our facilities and supplies are limited and help is a long way off. For example if someone needs to go hospital for tests it's a day's job, so one of us will take them, collect orders for shopping and return with a car full of goods."

Mary continued, "We swap any surplus we have like fruit or vegetables; someone will bring fish or game or a couple of chickens. I freeze and preserve many things and every fortnight we take items to the village hall to sell and swap for home baking, crafts, knitting and so on. We have soup and lunch there and a good old natter. Nobody wants to know your business, just know that you are well and not in need."

I told them of my welcoming experience at Acharacle and asked about social life. Rob was again very clear and direct,

"I believe that anywhere you live, especially as you age and have time on your hands, that you will be invited to do all manner of things. If you say 'No' then you are on the road to isolation. You have to make the effort, then, when you need a mechanic or someone to collect your prescription, help is always at hand."

These were sobering thoughts and I realised I could not cut

myself off from the world whilst waiting for a nuclear attack. Mary broke my thoughts,

"There is a Ceilidh tonight at the hotel, why not come along? It's a sort of barn dance or Highland fling but Ceilidh is Gaelic for a gathering or party."

"How can I say No?" Boy, what a night! They certainly know how to party! Dancing to a band; beer, lots of whisky, venison sausages and burgers, mussels, pasties, shortbread, Dundee Cake and Clootie Dumpling with cream. They don't appear to have licensing hours around here but it was pointed out that the only policeman was at the bar till it closed and beyond.

I rose late the next morning bleary-eyed and found that Mary had washed and ironed my clothes free of charge. I was preparing to leave that morning but Rob was outside with his dinghy on its trailer and a couple of fishing rods sticking out, so once again I decided not to say "No" accepting Rob's invitation to fish. We bobbed around in the bay on calmish water where the tips of the kelp seaweed peeped through the surface. Rob showed me how to float fish for Pollock and Cod patrolling the kelp forest in search of food. Sure enough, we caught enough to freeze and to swap, sell or giveaway. We soon had them filleted and it

was back to the cottage for shortbread and tea laced with whisky. Memories flooded back, chatting with Harold and Annie, river keepers on the River Dove in Derbyshire, and having an excess of "brown milk" until my lips and gums were numb.

The next morning I was genuinely saddened to leave Rob and Mary with warm handshakes and a long hug and kiss on the cheek from Mary. It had been an invaluable experience to gain knowledge about living and surviving in isolated communities and tempered my desire to live totally alone. Laide was a small community with a hotel, post office, filling station and caravan site so it was not for me, but I welcomed the short period of human company, conversation and the luxuries of home. I realised, however, that I would need such a community within shouting distance.

HEAVEN'S GATEWAY

I now had Little Loch Broom on my port side heading south to the end of the loch and exploring the north shore towards Scoraig, a settlement located on a remote peninsula. Again, the topography sent me back the way I had travelled to Dundonnell and the southern tip of the loch. Perusing my OS maps for some time and thinking about community support, hospital access and supplies, I looked to the east at Inverness where all would be available. The road went in one direction, southeast to join the A835 to Inverness on the east coast or west along the banks of Loch Broom to Ullapool.

Just north of this small town and ferry port, I had spotted a likely location on the River Eden. Turning left, I followed a sign down a narrow lane for Mains Farm props. A & M MacLeòid Gàradh Eden Estate. The lane wiggled gently downhill toward the coast and in front, I saw a woman struggling with a wooden crate and a garden fork.
"Can I give you a lift with that?" I enquired. The lady was in her forties, a mass of curly auburn hair and a ruddy complexion glowing with the exertion.

"Oh Hi. Thanks. I only went for a few potatoes for supper and got carried away. I'm only up the way there at the farm."

"Mrs MacLeòid?"

"Aye." She replied questioningly.

"I saw the name on the sign A & M MacLeòid proprietor."

"Oh aye, of course, my husband Angus. I am Morag." She informed holding out a hand. It was a rough strong hand formed by hard labour in a hard environment.

"Charles" I replied, feeling ashamed of my soft weak handshake. There was just room to get the crate in my sleeping compartment and I took her half a mile or so to the farmyard where an avalanche of dogs greeted us; two collies who lived in kennels in the yard, Midge the black Labrador and Jack the Jack Russell. A trio of farm cats, the rat and mouse catchers, kept their distance.

"Would you like a cup of tea? I am absolutely gasping for one!" enquired Morag almost imploring me to accept. Rob's advice never to say "No" immediately instructed my lips to accept. What opportunity may arise by saying yes, and I guessed Morag was in need of social interaction and some gossip to pass on to her friends about this English stranger. Morag was surprised at my taking tea black.

They kept a small dairy herd to supply the locality.

"We sell pasteurised full cream milk but we prefer our milk raw, unpasteurised." She informed. Having spotted my camping gear in the car, Morag was keen to know why I had chosen to turn into her lane terminating high on the moorland beyond. I was happy to tell most of my tale based on a bucket list of wild camping, free-swimming and fishing.

"My son, Murdo, is keen on fishing in the sea and in the loch up yonder." She advised lifting her eyes towards the high moorland behind the farm.

"If you want somewhere to camp then follow the lane about a mile until you come to a burn running through pipes under the road. There is a patch of grass there next to the shore and a small inlet with a jetty where you can fish. If you fancy a wee trout follow the burn up the brae to the lochan, especially in the evening, there are plenty of fish but they are only small about half to three quarters of a pound."

Manna from Heaven I thought. Could this be my idea of heaven? Thanking Morag for her hospitality, she followed me out to the car with a carrier bag. "You will need a bottle of milk and a couple of eggs for your breakfast." Putting a handful of new potatoes in the bag, she continued,

"Here, have these for dinner with your fish." I thanked her profusely for her kindness and generosity and proffered a fresh fish, yet to be caught, in exchange.

"Tight lines." She waved.

MacLeòid's Farm

The lane clung to the shoreline, a narrow band of grass, silver birch and rowan trees and a sandy beach. Shortly, I arrived at the burn and sure enough a lovely patch of bowling green grass shorn by the sheep who had left many calling cards on the green sward. My shovel soon scraped the area clean and Anja was parked nose to the west into the prevailing wind and weather. There was no sign of any bad weather as I pitched the awning in a slight balmy warm breeze. Looking through the tree line, the loch was almost a mirror and the burn gently trickled and bubbled into the rocky inlet Morag described.

Camp was quickly established, as I rushed to catch the tide edging up the shoreline. I yearned to start fishing but priorities are always; shelter first, water, fire then food. At the lane side a pipe from the burn drained into a small stone trough covered in moss and lined with aquatic plants. Such roadside troughs are quite common to quench the thirst of the traveller, livestock and wildlife. It was cool and crystal clear and probably safe to drink but I would boil it to be safe. I had food but fresh fish instead of dry pasta was my preferred menu. The pasta was for emergencies.

The burn fell quietly into a narrow grassy inlet where wind and tide had created a wood-store of flotsam and jetsam conveniently left high and dry on the banks. A fallen birch tree provided oil rich bark for tinder that I would ignite from my yet untested Ray Mears firestick. Now I could explore and fish.

Beyond the burn a narrow cart track ran from the road and along the side of the inlet. The track narrowed to a horizontal path cut into the rock face on the offside, but falling down to the shore and deeper water to the nearside. The inlet gradually widened and about thirty yards in, were the remains of a floating pontoon, three to four yards from the shore. A gangway connected the top of the pontoon to the shore, hinged by chains allowing for the rise and fall of the tides. The track terminated at the gangplank with a small turning circle. Tentatively, I walked the gangplank with no handrails but the wooden boards seemed to be sound. The pontoon, also boarded with wood over a metal box, was anchored to the seabed in quite deep water, probably to allow boats to load and unload. Looking out over the loch, I saw that the inlet widened considerably, but my view beyond the turning circle was obscured by the hillside descending steeply to the shoreline. A path clung to the edge disappearing around the corner that was in need of future exploration.

Pollack

Time to fish. In the clear water, I could see kelp forest, a sign of nutrient-rich water and an ideal habitat for many marine species especially Pollock, my target fish, cruising within the long kelp stems. Tips of the plants broke the surface tension indicating the extent of this underwater woodland. My chosen tackle was a mussel plucked fresh from the shore suspended below a float to drift through the stems, hopefully without snagging. I sat on my folding angler's chair breathing the warm salty air, basking in the early afternoon sun, watching the colours and reflections, sun glinting off the wavelets. I was in seventh heaven a phrase we often use without knowing its meaning or origin. Google records a Chinese takeaway in Neath and the venue for Glasgow's premier lap dancing club! Collins dictionary suggests that I was in a state of complete happiness. Suddenly, a sheepdog on the end of the gangplank, rudely interrupted my silent contemplation. Barking to tell me of its presence it crouched, tail wagging furiously, lips smiling and bright eyes yearning for signs of a response. A "hello" from me was all that was required as she shot along the plank locking herself into my side, ramming her head under my arm and washing my cheek with her tongue.

"Jess. Jessie."

Looking to my left, I saw a tall slender figure trotting along the track towards me. Her bounding step instantly reduced to a cautious tentative walk keeping a safe distance and weighing me up. Who was this stranger? Was I a threat? She had to make contact as her dog was glued to my side. She started with an apology for Jessie's behaviour and tried to call her back, but Jessie was having none of it.

"I think she has taken a liking to me." I offered.

"Yes, it does, which is rather odd because she is normally very wary of men."

I guess she was mid to late fifties, slim, attractive, her long strawberry-blonde hair tied back with a simple strand of cotton fabric. Apart from gold stud earrings, there was neither jewellery apparent nor tattoos. With such a tanned complexion, she had no need of makeup accentuating her brilliant white smile. She wore a calf length floral pattern dress deep V neckline buttoned down the front. Her shoes seemed rather old-fashioned, being dark brown leather brogues, thick leather soles and, judging by the noise, metal studs or skegs. They were well-worn but polished and cared for, her ankle socks, once white, now greyed a little with age, and turned over.

I felt rather awkward pinned to my angling chair while wrestling with the over-friendly Jessie. Putting my rod down, I crawled to my feet with Jessie now pressing hard against my right calf. Her actions brought back wonderful childhood memories of being on holiday in Edale at the end of the Pennine Way. Every day this five year old would leave our cottage, team up with a collie from the farm, and go on adventures, totally unsupervised and without any fear of strangers. How life has changed.

She stepped back from the gangway

as I ambled across removing my cap and offering my hand.

"As we have no one to make an introduction, I'm Charles." She cautiously took my hand briefly at arm's length, keeping her distance.

"Penny, and of course you know Jessie." We both laughed. Penny had a lovely warm smile

and kind gentle laughing eyes. It was time for some awkward small talk.

"Erm. I am wild camping just by the burn there." Nodding towards Anja.

"Yes, I assumed that was your camp. I live in the croft over the lane." She revealed perhaps regretting she had given away too much information. Once again, I explained my mission to survive in the wilds of Scotland, camp, catch fish, enjoy the freedom and solitude, escape the city life and find a place of my own, not a holiday let, something more permanent especially if Putin sets the world alight in a nuclear World War Three.

Penny looked rather thoughtful and quizzical at my mention of nuclear war but her expression changed suddenly as she pointed excitedly towards the jetty shouting.

"Look out! Your rod is sliding away."

Sure enough, the rod was drifting along the pontoon, the reel catching in a lashing point as

my float and line were heading out to sea! Managing to clamber over Jessie, I retrieved the rod to strike as the fish tugged away in the kelp forest. It was a good heavy fish pulling and diving in attempts to escape but he was well hooked, gradually losing power and floating to the surface, splashing in one last-ditch attempt, before rolling, spent, on his side.

"Penny! Could you help please? Could you pass the net?" Penny leapt to my aid deftly scooping the Pollock into the net.

"You've done that before. Most expert. Thank heavens you saw my rod disappearing. I would have had to dive in after it!"

Penny turned away as I delivered the last rites to the fish and removed the hook. She was wiping her eyes.

"I'm sorry Penny. I did not mean to upset you by dealing with the fish."

"No. No. It's not that. I have netted fish many times, here on this jetty for my father, and I was reminded of him and the times we had together here."

Nodding sympathetically, I offered a clean white handkerchief, one that Mary had washed, ironed and folded.

"Penny. This is a big fish. Far too much for my needs. If I fillet it, would you like some for yourself, for the freezer perhaps."

"That's most kind. Yes, please I would. Thank you."

As Penny bent down to put Jessie on her lead, it was noticeable that Penny had nothing on under her dress and I was gentlemanly enough to avert my gaze.

"I see you have a towel. Are you going for a swim?"

"Erm. Ye.... er no It's for Jessie she goes in the water so I give her a rub down before we get home and shakes all over the house." She replied rather unconvincingly. If she was going swimming and if she was topless or even naked then she would be uncomfortable, insecure with my presence.

"Pollock tend to shoal so it's worth me carrying on until the tide turns about an hour or so I would guess. I will fillet this one for you and you can pick it up on your way back."

Penny seemed much relieved and with a, "See you soon then." set off with the spring returning to her steps and disappeared on the path round the edge of the rocks. I tried to concentrate on my newly baited line but Penny had made a significant impact on me. I was right about the shoal and landed two more before I heard those skegs striking the stony path. Penny looked different, slightly dishevelled, her hair wet and no longer held back by the cotton strip. I guessed she had been swimming.

"I have two more. I thought I would take one to Morag at the farm, as she was kind enough to give me potatoes, eggs and milk. I can fillet the other for your freezer."

"I'm sure Morag and Angus would appreciate the fish and I have to see Morag so I could nip down on my bike, if you like."

"Yes, by all means, please do. It is always best eaten fresh anyway."

Penny nodded and smiled while I gathered my courage to ask her a question, the sort of question that on many occasions I have been unable to ask and subsequently regretted. "Penny, I know we have only just met, and I hope that you would not think it presumptuous of me to invite you to have dinner with me this evening, at the camp…..I cannot eat all of it myself….."

I wanted to keep on talking to delay the inevitable negative response…… "I have this marvellous recipe for baked Pollock with a crispy bread, herb and parmesan crust……would you share it with me?"

Penny was clearly taken aback but maybe she had been advised of Rob's philosophy of saying 'No' leading to isolation.

"Well I have nothing in my social diary tonight so I would be delighted to dine chez camp." She laughed.

"Shall we say six? That gives me time for a swim in my bath and get the fire going. I don't have a pudding though, but I do have a rather good Chablis or Sancerre I can put in the chiller. Which would you prefer?"

"Oh Sancerre sounds wonderful. See you at six then." Whereupon she turned sharply on her heel and skipped off up the track.

Dutch Oven

Panic stations. What had I done? The fish was soon prepared on a base of foil ready for my Dutch oven. I gathered sticks and logs by the fire pit I dug on the shore, surrounded by large stones. The oven was suspended on a tripod I had made at the local Men's Shed and was soon warming over the early flames. All was ready apart from me so, stripping off to my pants I launched myself with great enthusiasm and abandon into the loch, then back to the privacy of my awning to change. Raiding my larder I prepared a starter, mixing flour, yeast and water for crispy bread rolls. I was ready to impress a lady with my camping table, no cloth or napkins, but metal knives and forks, two metal enamel plates, white with a navy blue ring, matching mugs and two plastic tumblers. The Sancerre lay in the water nearby. Panic when I could not find the corkscrew but it came to hand eventually. The fire had now died down so I set the Dutch oven on the embers with my dough balls inside, placed the lid and shovelled further embers on top to provide downward heat.

Jessie's rapturous greeting was the first I knew of Penny's approach and I turned to see a beautiful woman approaching, a stylishly coiffeured woman, pearl drop earrings, a hint of delicately-shaded lipstick, her tanned complexion almost matching her strawberry blonde hair falling in tresses onto her shoulders. Her golden silk blouse sporting long extensions of the collar tied in a loose knot, was paired with slim-fitting black trousers and glittery sandals. She was elegance and sophistication personified.

I had done the best I could from my limited wardrobe and in any case, I had to cook and maintain the fire.

"Good evening Madame and welcome to Chez Camp. Would you like this table by the loch?" A smile was creeping across her face, her bright white teeth gleaming from her tanned complexion.

"I think you will find this seat more comfortable than the commode Madame." We both burst into laughter, as she looked at my camping toilet stool resplendent with a cushion. I reassured Penny that I had given it a good wash in the loch.

"Is that fresh bread I can smell?"

"It is indeed. We have olives with fresh crusty rolls and an olive oil and balsamic vinegar dip. I hope that will be ok?"

"It will indeed. Yes most impressive." Penny proclaimed with perhaps a hint of admiration.

"I will just fetch the Sancerre from the chiller." I advised, strolling to the water's edge where my bottle was cooling. A wipe with a clean towel, a pop of the cork and the wine gurgled into the plastic glasses.

"That is so good. We don't get wine like this easily up here Charles. It takes me right back to Harrod's wine bar for an early evening drink after work. But here, in these surroundings it is certainly something else."

So far, I felt the evening was going rather well as I removed the lid from the Dutch oven to envelope us in a cloud of fresh steamy bread aroma that Penny breathed in deeply.

"Oh wonderful." She sighed.

With bread on the table, I placed the Pollock with its bread and parmesan herb crust in the oven and set a pan of Morag's new potatoes in sea water on the Trangia stove.

"I am short of napkins but I do have clean tea towels." I advised, as I unfolded and draped a towel across her lap. Tucking into our bread and olives with great relish, I enquired about her employment in London.

"Oh I was in publishing, started as a proof reader and then editor and made my way up to director."

"What sort of material?" I asked with great interest given my creative writing attempts. "Celebrity biographies and romantic novels mainly……" and Penny continued to talk easily about her work for some time….. "Listen at me going on. I am doing all the talking."

"I am a good listener Penny and it is all very interesting…" and I proceeded to describe my literary achievements with a particular emphasis on The Hidden Glen until the alarm on my mobile signalled time to check the main course.

"I'm afraid we will have to use the same plates as I only have the two."

"Saves washing up" approved Penny. I tested the potatoes before scooping them onto the plates with a slotted spoon. Once again, the Dutch oven was producing a delightful aroma as I lifted the foil base onto the table. The crust was now toasted golden brown with a crispy crunch and beneath a pure white moist fillet of soft flakes.

"Done to a turn I think Penny. I apologise for just the one vegetable but I'm afraid I am right out of samphire and asparagus. Perhaps you would like butter or olive oil on your potatoes." "I think I will crush them with a little oil like all the best TV chefs."

"Is it Penny or Penelope?"

"Oh christened Penelope but always been called Penny."

"I think I prefer Penny. I had a traumatic experience with a Penelope…..as a child at junior school. We were reading parts in a play and I came in about halfway through with my first line, which included 'Penelope', but it came out as 'Penny lope.' We had to start from the beginning but it was 'Penny lope' again. The teacher was not amused, thinking I was being mischievous. The third time she tore the book from my hand and I sat there in silent ignominy. Never had a problem since but I am still pleased you are Penny."

Though I say so myself, the fish was fantastic, perhaps enhanced by the salty breeze coming in from the loch.

"Morag was delighted with the Pollock and thanks you for your kindness."

"Well Penny, fair exchange is no robbery, and I appreciate just how essential it is for people in isolated communities with limited resources to share what they have." I went on to tell her about my experience at the community hall in Acharacle and with Rob and Mary in Laide. Penny agreed that getting away from the city and the rat race is something many desire but the reality of isolation is sometimes a bitter pill to swallow. I asked her if she had seen Bob Mortimer and Paul Whitehouse on Gone Fishing and in particular, the episode where Bob philosophised saying 'No is a pathway to isolation watching television in a bungalow.'

Penny's face seemed to drop as if I had struck a chord with her.

"What he was saying, is that when we get asked out, or to do something, it is easier to say 'No' and we should embrace every opportunity late in life."

Penny nodded, "Yes you are right it is so easy to lock yourself away."

I felt that I dared not delve deeper sensing that perhaps she may have locked herself away. Changing tack, I asked about her tears when she helped land the fish and referred to her father.

"Oh it was just that you took me back to the seventies when we had holidays here in the croft and we sailed and fished, we walked the glens and the beach and swam in the loch. They were wonderful idyllic days."

"So how did you find this place?"

"That's a long story……."

"Have another glass of wine and I will make fresh coffee. I regret I have no petit fours!"

Penny seemed to come out of her sad moment proceeding to tell me that father had been a senior civil servant in the MOD at the time of the Cuban crisis and the Cold War. There was serious concern about the effects of a nuclear attack and the safety of the Royal Family so father was asked to draft an operational order to evacuate them, first to obscure country houses in Scotland and to the Royal Yacht Britannia hiding in the lochs on the west coast."

"Operation Candid." I interrupted.

Penny was clearly taken aback,

"Yes! Yes! That's right but how did you know that?"

"Wikipedia. I was looking at the potential threat from Putin and Ukraine and came across Operation Candid and the likely targets in the UK. However, what is more important to me is the unlikely targets in the UK. What I mean is where would be the safest place to survive a nuclear attack?"

Penny seemed relieved at my explanation but left her still

wondering.

"So your father implemented the plan?"

"The sporting lodge at the top of the lane here was identified as about the most secluded and isolated property available but within easy reach of Inverness airport if the Royals had to be flown to Canada for example. Loch Broom was also the ideal spot to hide the royal yacht. The MOD bought the croft to house military personnel operating a signals and observation post and created the jetty for tenders to drop off stores and passengers."

"How interesting."

"Father said they had to use explosives to excavate the track and then the pontoon was dropped from a navy ship and towed into the inlet. Father spent a lot of time up here supervising work at the lodge and fell in love with the area."

"So what happened when the Cold War came to an end in the late eighties?"

"The lodge was returned to the owners and the croft was forgotten about by the MOD until father suggested it could be sold and he bought it."

"And you now live here permanently?" I enquired seeking her reasons for leaving London, a good job and salary. Was it a man or several men, broken relationships perhaps? Then it struck me that in these LGBGT plus times it could have been a different type of relationship. "Pretty much, yes. I still have my flat in London that I rent out but I have always had the happiest times of my life here, so it was the obvious choice when I felt the need to leave so-called civilisation and lead my own version of a peaceful and civilised life."

I nodded my understanding and she continued to explain that when father passed she cared for mother and worked a lot from home until she also passed five years ago. I miss them terribly. I became bored and irritated with celebrity egotistical biographies and I suppose I was drawn to romantic novels where people live their dreams. This was my dream. Father left me the croft so here I am."

"You have good friends here?"

"Yes, not many obviously, but Morag and Angus at the farm; Davy and his wife Sue; who live further up near the lodge. He is the estate stalker and general handyman so he has all the big boys' toys like chainsaws and a tractor. The gamekeeper and ghillie, Alex and wife Isla live out on the hill so I see less of them. Between them, Angus and Davy can clear the lane if we are snowed in and help me with logs for the fire. Morag is a good friend to chat with although there is not much gossip hereabouts, not until you arrived! You can bet the stranger will be the centre of attention."

"I'm sure I will be an enigma until they get to know more about me."

"Sue is housekeeper at the lodge. The owners live down south and visit in late autumn to stalk, fish and shoot grouse, like the old days. The rest of the time the lodge and the estate are let to parties for sporting or hill walking, bird watching, photography groups.... we even had a group of ladies doing cold-water therapy, yoga and free swimming. They would jog past each morning and evening in their lycra and ankle socks."

"So there is a lot more activity here than one would expect?"

"Yes in short bursts, after three or four days or a week they race back like lemmings to the metropolis and their busy lives. I hope I don't sound too critical of them as their money keeps the lodge going, employment for the estate, Angus sells them his produce so they do have a wide financial impact on the whole area."

I nodded approvingly.

"For some groups I help out with art classes, taking them to paint on the shore or in the glen. I also put Sue in touch with literary groups who come to write, like the Jane Austen Society or Lovers of Dickins, I do book readings and give a talk about celebrity biographies, they seem to like a bit of star studded gossip."

"Penny. My limited larder does not extend to a dessert other than some well travelled Dundee Cake and an open packet of shortbread." I apologised.

Reaching for her shoulder bag Penny replied,

"I took the liberty of bringing some local cheese, a rather strong Scottish cheddar." Placing a packet on the table before reaching in again, "my homemade damson cheese, and a bottle of my damson gin." she smiled looking for my approval.

"I think you must be Mary Poppins! Who would have guessed that two total strangers could have met and produced such a fine feast out of nothing in the middle of nowhere? We need fresh plates." I continued rising from my converted commode and washing the enamel dinner plates in the loch.

The damson gin was warming but I noticed Penny shiver as the sun disappeared over the horizon leaving only the residual warmth from the fire.

"What are your plans for tomorrow?" She enquired.

"I think I would like to explore the coast beyond the jetty, look at fishing spots as I guess there must be salmon and sea trout hereabouts, go for a swim, do my domestic chores, collect wood for the fire and think of something for dinner. Quite a busy day don't you think?"

"I can show you the coastline, swimming and fishing spots if you like, and I would love to return your hospitality with dinner at the Croft.

"Manna from heaven Penny. Never say no as Bob Mortimer says."

Penny rose to leave,

"Thank you for such a wonderful evening, not just the superb food but your company and conversation."

"The pleasure was all mine Penny."

Pausing in the glow of the fire, her eyes sparkled in the flickering flames. How I wanted to kiss her goodnight, just a peck on the cheek, a mwah. But would that ruin the evening?

"Let me help you back to the road." I said, offering a hand that she took readily as far as the tarmac before releasing her grip.

"Goodnight then. See you in the morning. Come on Jessie." and with that she strolled into the darkness with a brief glimpse back and a wave.

What a night! What a woman! Now back to reality, clear the table, wash the pots, store the commode and climb into bed, perchance to dream.

Breakfast was leftover bread and fried potato and egg. Not exactly, cordon bleu but a good start to the day for an explorer. I found an ideal location about twenty yards away along the shore where I could secrete the commode and myself. Hidden in the bushes I could sit with a mug of Earl Grey and look out to sea. Quite an enlightening and life enhancing experience, and no need for the plastic bag, after digging a deep hole for my latrine and covering my you know what with sand and soil. Now time to freshen up with a fully clothed quick dip and a bar of soap laundering both myself and my shirt and pants. The Trangia kettle whistled that my shaving water was ready. A clean shirt and shorts set me up for the expedition. Again, Jessie was the early indication of Penny's approach rolling on her back in total submission before planting herself firmly at my side seeking as much attention as I could give her.

"Is the flag at half mast?" Penny laughed, pointing at my laundry blowing on a line strung between two Scot's pine trees.

"It's a signal. England expects that Charles will enjoy his

expedition with Penny, oh and you Jessie."

I noted there was plenty of firewood by the burn as we crossed on to the track. Penny was an informative guide explaining how father had designed and built it recounting many happy memories from their family holidays.

At the turning circle, the track became a path clinging to the rock face with a steep grassy bank dropping sharply to the water's edge. The cliff side curved away to the right and the path descended to a sandy silver beach of pure soft sand.

"We call it whistling sand from the noise it makes under your feet."

Tràigh Pàrras, Paradise Beach showing the river pool far right and "changing room rocks" in the centre. The jetty and inlet is off the picture to the left.

The crystal clear, caribbean-esque blue water rolled gently against the rocky shoreline creating a pure white foamy ribbon.

The rocky cliff gave way to sloping hillside covered in a bright green swathe of grass kept at bowling-green length by the sheep, dotted with daisies and a myriad of wild flowers. Patches of flowering yellow gorse punctuated the slopes before giving way to bracken and heather. At high tide, the sea enveloped the grass fringes creating pools and rivulets full of small creatures, fish and crabs. I stood in wonder viewing the most idyllic beach. I noted Penny watching my reaction and smiling,

"Traigh Parras, Paradise Beach. It is wonderful isn't it? Mostly I think this is all mine. Only rarely, is my ownership challenged by a visiting small yacht but they are soon gone."

"So the only access is by boat or the path from the jetty?" She nodded in affirmation.

The view from my campsite was mainly open water of a wide circular bay with an island at is entrance, but at this point, the end of the loch curved to meet the river at the far end rather like an estuary.

"This is a great place for beach combing. I can always find; driftwood, shells, fishing gear and so on that I collect to do something arty or crafty with. I also clear whatever I can to keep it pristine."

The far side of the estuary rose sharply from the sea, no sand just a rocky edge and covered in gorse, bracken and a few hardy bushes and windblown thorn trees. In places, large gnarled fingers of rock pierced the beach as if some mighty hand sought to grab a handful of sand and carry it away, but it was too fine and soft to handle.

"This is where I come to swim.," said Penny and these rocks are my changing rooms. I realised now that yesterday Penny had been swimming here and her comments about Jessie were a defensive smoke screen. Jessie was quite happy paddling and cavorting in the water's edge retrieving stones and shells for Penny and her new found friend.

Beyond the changing rooms, the beach narrowed to the river flowing steadily down a steep sided gorge progressing through a series of pools and broken water to mingle its peat-tinged water with the salt of the loch.

"The lodge is named after the river, Gàradh Eden, Garden of Eden."

We sat for some time quietly watching the pool where the waters met. I was looking for signs of fish, probably sea trout at this time of year ready to run the river to the redds, shallow gravelly beds to lay their eggs. Penny pointed to a seal rolling in the loch.

"I think there is a family of otters on that far bank."

"What about sea eagles. I understand they have made a comeback?"

"I have seen large birds flying over the loch that may be sea eagles and Alex sees Golden Eagles on the moor."

Highland Cattle on the beach

Turning to observe the grassy slope, I saw a handful of Angus MacLeòid's Highland Cattle grazing and a line of red deer moving across the skyline.

"Sometimes you see the cattle eating seaweed, or chewing the cud while sunbathing on the beach, and in winter the deer come right down the Glen even to the shore in search of food and raid my garden. Sadly, there is insufficient food for the population and they are poor looking things when they starve. People pay the estate to stalk deer but they have little impact on the numbers. Davy culls through the seasons but it is a tremendous task for one man to maintain a viable population and they raid Angus' crops at the farm. In the woods, you can see Red Squirrel and occasionally the elusive Pine Martin. He is the thief in the night clearing anything left on the bird tables."

I was keen to explore the river gorge and the pool at its mouth, where a reasonable current projected into the loch leaving a brown peaty stain. It looked ideal for fishing a fly, a wee double in the late evening and a larger single hooked teal blue and silver in the wee small hours when the big fish may be tempted to take. The flow was also strong enough to carry a small spoon on the spinning rod for sea trout or flat fish. It was an easy walk up the steadily rising riverbank. The bed was a mass of small boulders on a sandy gravelly base and the occasional big lump of rock. The pools were quite deep, perhaps five or six feet in places where the river had scoured and gouged the bed out. There would be small brown trout in there that eventually migrate to the briny water of the loch growing into strong-fighting wary sea trout. The depth of the pools allowed salmon to leap the shallow falls on their way to the redds. It was all most promising. I returned to the fingers of rock but Penny had vanished. Looking between two of the fingers I saw her towel and clothes. Jessie had seen me and bounded up with a welcoming bark.

"Come on in! Join me for a swim."

I didn't want to say no but I had not brought my swimming shorts. Speedos were a thing of my youth and don't look at all attractive on an older portly person.

"I haven't got my swimming trunks!" I responded.

"Neither have I!" responded Penny laughing.

Who could resist such an invitation? Immediately recalling Ben Fogle getting the same invitation from a naked blonde lady in a lake. Both managed to behave themselves as the underwater camera caught them with the merest flashes of bodily parts. If it was good enough for Ben then it was good enough for me. Stripping off in the rocks, I decided to make a rapid running entrance rather than a slow pedestrian one to minimise the shock of seeing my un-athletic torso. The water was certainly as cold as I anticipated even under the hot afternoon sun, but I was soon "Fogleing," diving and porpoise rolling whilst maintaining a discreet distance from Penny. It was difficult to avert my eyes especially when she came within a few yards before turning and diving with a flash of bare bottom and splashing me with her feet like a mermaid's tail.

I saw her making for the shore, rising naked, statuesque from the water like a goddess or a model in one of those perfume adverts that seem to have little or no meaning. My son says they don't need a meaning they are just a portrayal of an aspiration. I could aspire to jumping in a Greek temple bath with a dozen naked models, but climbing a ship's mast with Jean Paul Gaultier or playing a guitar like Johnny Depp in a desert surrounded by wolves is not something I aspire to. My predicament was like a scene from a Carry On film where the girls, Barbara Windsor perhaps, had stolen my clothes. I could just brave it and walk resolutely up the beach or like a mouse with my hands covering my embarrassment. Penny saved the day. Now dressed, she walked into the shallows carrying an outstretched towel laughing.

"Come on I won't look or drop the towel. Promise."

What a minx, but I gladly accepted the towel ensuring the gentlest touches of her hands as we exchanged grip. Having dressed we laughed and talked. She also pointed out where I could do the mobile phone waltz, my quizzical look demanding an explanation.

"That rock on the top of the grassy slope is where you might get a signal but you have to do the waltz, you hold the phone in the air and dance about until it pings."

I nodded and smiled my understanding.

"I think you have to get in line with a signal on the other side of the bay. Sometimes it works. Lunch?" She asked.

I had never thought about lunch. I had nothing prepared and no bread.

"Lunch in the garden? A sandwich and cake sound ok?"

It certainly was ok. The Croft was about fifty yards above my roadside campsite. Surprisingly it was out of view due to the rock face but further on a drive cut through the wall rising to a grassy plateau and the Croft set back against rising ground, benefitting from the southern aspect and protection from the north wind. A red Mini Countryman sat by the front door located in the middle of the single white rendered cottage. Stone walls and wire livestock netting set out the boundary to keep out the sheep and lower small mesh rabbit netting sought to protect a vegetable plot and poly tunnel. A trio of beehives filled a far corner of the plot and a wooden table and chairs on the lawn, provided a magnificent vantage point over the bay and the island.

"I have homemade lemonade if you are thirsty."

"Yes, please I am rather thirsty from the salt."

Penny appeared from the Croft with a tray and jug of lemonade.

"I have some cold beef and chutneys. My bread is from the freezer, but it is sourdough."

"That sounds just the job Penny." and she skipped away to the kitchen re-emerging with a plate of sliced beef, mustard, horseradish and damson chutney.

"I thought we might have the cheese again as well."

Over lunch, Penny filled me in on more of the history of the area but I was keen to know more about Operation Candid.

"Did the royals ever make it here and what did the soldiers do?"

"Operation Candid included a detachment to guard the Queen and about eight were based here to secure access by road to the lodge. I gather they patrolled in a Landrover and carried pistols and machine guns. There was concern because at another location down south a Russian naval attaché had been seen observing. To keep the lodge as secret as possible, father had the lodge and croft deleted from OS maps and changed the name of the river to Eden.

The soldiers were very friendly, getting to know the locals who would act as early warning if strangers were on the prowl. They were very free with bottles of whisky, tobacco and cigarettes so were always made welcome. They were always keen to give away large tins of bully beef in exchange for a salmon or a chicken or Morag's mother's fruitcake. There were aerials on that pole for communications and father said they monitored western approaches for foreign language transmissions from ships and kept watch for Russian spy trawlers. Apparently, they drove a track across the moor in their Landrover to the river and had a shelter overlooking the ocean."

"I would like to walk that one day. Sounds very interesting."

"Some supplies came by road but a naval ship would anchor in the bay using a tender to deliver whatever was needed for the post and the lodge. I don't think the lodge was ever used by the royals but there are tales of some memorable parties with lots of free booze that were well attended by those hereabouts. The Croft had two bedrooms with four bunks in each. Father soon got rid of those on the fire and furnished the Croft to be warm and comfortable. We came here every summer for several weeks. Dad took his annual leave but would visit various defence establishments across Scotland for several days at a time returning with a car full of NAAFI goods to keep us going."

Penny paused pensively,

"They were great times. A very happy period in my life.....so this evening I would like to return your hospitality with a meal here. How does fillet of venison sound?"

"Absolutely, spot on. Can I provide the wine? I do have an excellent red."

"By all means. My cellar is mostly homemade plum and damson. Shall we say seven?"

I floated back to Anja at the campsite on cloud nine unable to believe my experiences over the last two days. The camp needed some maintenance and tidying, gathering a good store of firewood, preparation of dry tinder and kindling especially the oily birch bark for lighting. My bed needed an airing so it replaced my dry clothing on the line. My shirts felt and smelt remarkably clean and not badly creased but I felt the need to make an effort and an impression that evening. I had packed my Bladen tweed jacket described by Carters of Helmsley as "The Bladen Original jacket paired with flannels and cord trousers, provides the flexibility to handle the vast majority of social situations." Should fit the bill then with open neck shirt and House of Bruar Donegal salt and pepper check trousers and brown brogues. Pure sartorial, elegance from the boot of a car.

What about disguising my rather salty odour? Time for a stand up wash in the washing up bowl with burn water, soap and flannel. Trangia could only supply a pan of hot water but enough to provide some warm comfort in all parts. Swill down with an enamel mug and I was done, apart from dabbing a spot of gentlemanly aftershave here and there. In my youth, Our Henry Cooper did the business dropping Cassius Clay in the boxing ring so splashing Brut on all over was de rigueur. Now that I am more of a salty old sea dog I think Old Spice would be more appropriate and perhaps evoke a memory or two.

I was ready but it was only 6pm. I had peaked too early so I sat and discussed the meaning of life with Anja while listening to the state of the world on her radio. 6.55pm, adjust shirt pulling it out round the belt to disguise my overhanging belly, slip on the Bladen complete with a British Legion poppy pocket-handkerchief. "Wish me luck Anja." as I flicked her locks in case of a sudden but unlikely crime wave. Jessie sounded my arrival as I crunched up the drive. Penny was at the door to greet me with a smile.

"My oh my. You do scrub up well."

"You don't look so bad yourself Penny."

Penny was just as glamorous as the previous evening in a black cocktail dress, exposed shoulders and elegant form, and high heels, her hair tied back in a bun. I am no fashionista, but the dress was reminiscent of the iconic "revenge dress" worn by Princess Diana after her divorce from Prince Charles. It didn't look like this Charles was facing a divorce tonight.

"Come in. Dinner is nearly ready. Take a seat by the fire."

I brought a bottle of red. I hope you like it, Margaux."

"Margaux! Most certainly I do. Can you uncork it and let it breathe by the fire."

I pointed to Jessie laid across my feet. Penny handed the bottle and corkscrew and returned to the kitchen. With my feet pinned to the floor I could only sit and scan the living room, a warm cosy room lit by one small window, the glowing fire and a small lamp in the corner sitting on a bookcase. I guessed the contents were books she had published judging by the celebrity names leaping out of the spines. Of greater interest were several unframed canvases featuring seascapes and one in particular of the beach below. She certainly had a talent. Above the fireplace hung a portrait of a man and a woman, her parents perhaps.

"Come on through and bring the wine please."

"I will if Jessie lets me."

Jessie leapt to Penny's call as I followed into the dining kitchen a simple room, butler sink wooden draining board seventies style cupboards and a freestanding electric cooker with eye level grill. The dining table was set with a linen cloth, cut glass, a candle and gold-rimmed white china plates. Penny stood behind her chair gauging my response. I nodded and smiled, "All this and proper chairs as well."

"I don't have a commode," she laughed.

A plate of venison medallions cooked pink with a steaming bowl of new potatoes and green beans came to her table.

"For your delectation this evening Charles, we have Pommes de Morag, haricots verts,
seared venison medallions in a wild bramble and juniper sauce with foraged mushrooms. "That looks absolutely splendid Penny. I think we could open a restaurant."

"There's not a great call in these parts for fine dining except for the clients at the lodge."

We shared the washing up before settling in front of the fire with a damson gin.

"Oh Penny what a wonderful day we have had."

Penny settled back in her armchair sighing,

"Yes indeed we have."

We talked about her celebrities and their biographies but my real interest was in her paintings, all local land and seascapes, watercolours with moody atmospheric lighting.

" Are these your parents?"

"Yes. I painted them from a photograph when I moved up here. I felt it helped me to grieve and keep them alive in my memory.

The people we love will always live on in our memories of the good times we had with them."

My hand dropped over the arm of my chair to be met by the ever-present Jessie.

"She really has taken to you. It is strange because she is very wary of most men. She tolerates Angus and Davy but keeps a cautious distance. My father was the only man she would go to for a fuss."

The fire died to a few glowing embers and wisps of blue smoke but in the firelight, I caught a glimpse of wetness in her eyes as she rose to draw the curtain behind my chair. I sensed her behind me as her hand rested on my shoulder moving slowly across my back, a finger stroking my bare neck as she bent over touching her cheek against my ear. Taking my left hand in her left hand, she whispered,

"Charles….this is not a time to say no."

I awoke the next morning to find the bed was empty and cold but I could hear the sounds of domesticity ringing from the kitchen. Drawing back the floral duvet revealed my nakedness, reflecting briefly before Penny entered the room.

"Good morning!" she chirped cheerfully, "Tea?"

"Oh morning Penny. Yes please." I croaked.

Placing the mug on the bedside cabinet, she bent over placing a kiss on my cheek that I was not quick enough to return. Picking a fresh towel from a chair, she dropped it on the bed indicating the shower in the room next door.

"Scrambled eggs on toast ok for breakfast?"

I managed a 'Yes please.' while slurping from my hot mug of tea. "Won't be long."

A flushing toilet felt luxurious after my camping commode and a hot soapy shower was bliss. Nipping back to the bedroom modestly attired in a wet towel I slipped into my underpants and straightened the bed out as neatly as I could. I plumped up Penny's pillows smelling her fragrance as my mind raced through a repeat of our night together.

"Ready on the table!" interrupted my reflection.

"I thought I would dress for breakfast...." I joked "....as I seem to have come without any clothes." We laughed and engaged in a warm embrace.

"What's on the cards for today?"

"Well this evening a party is arriving at the lodge for a painting weekend so I normally help Sue and Isla with the meal. I also do a short presentation about the area and send the weary travellers off to bed. Then, tomorrow I spend the morning with them painting.

"Can I help with the meal, waiting on, or washing up?"

"That would be much appreciated. You could be the sommelier."

"I need to go and change into my working clothes as I only have one set of posh best."

"Why don't you decamp all together and bring Anja up here. She can chat with Millie the Mini. There is plenty of space in the wardrobe in the spare room for your clothes. PJs on my bed though!" she instructed cheekily plonking a warm kiss on my lips.

Penny was obviously in no mood to be argued with, and what man, especially this one, would want to change her mind anyway? I almost jogged back to camp packing everything away as quickly as possible so I could return to my new life. In no more than half an hour, I took down the clothesline, filled in the latrine, covered the campfire with fresh sand and cleared the site. Anja fired up immediately probably relieved at getting back to normal, relieved at not being abandoned on the loch shore. I apologised for my overnight absence and I am sure there was a shrugged acceptance as she changed gear.

Parking bonnet to bonnet with Millie the Mini I began removing my clothes and personal effects. Penny came out to help with a tray of coffee and shortbread and we bathed in the warm morning sun holding hands. Penny suggested I take a stroll, more like an expedition, along the track to the observation point, turn left at the top of the hill and follow the wheel marks through the heather to the river.

"The vehicle crossing may have been washed out so take a stick to help across the boulders then follow the tracks again to a stone bothy. I'm sure Jessie would like to go with you on the lead perhaps then let her off on the track. If she runs off she will only come back here. Oh and you might want to try the mobile phone waltz at the big rock. There is bread and cheese in the kitchen. Help yourself, and I will see you any time after 3pm. Oh, bring Jessie with you. They dine about six. I will cycle it's about two miles but you could take the car if you wish.

"That's fine. Best bib and tucker. See you there."

MEETING THE LOCALS

For an isolated sparsely populated place that didn't even have a name, life in the last twenty four hours had been most eventful and getting even more hectic. Gentle reader; please do not get me wrong I ain't complaining!

Jessie lay on the mat at the front door looking doleful and declining my invitations to come to me for a bit of fuss but soon leapt to her toes when I hooked her lead from the door. Now she had her front paws on my thigh yearning for the lead around her neck and we were off. I just needed to find the key to lock up but it was nowhere to be found. Perhaps security was unheard of in these parts. Taking a thumb stick from the milk churn by the door, we set off, Jessie trotting at my side leaning slightly into her lead and eager to reach the top of the hill. From here, the ground levelled into heather moorland dotted with an odd hawthorn tree, stunted and contorted in to strange shapes by the prevailing winds. The wheel tracks in the heather took us over the moor. Jessie looked at me seeking her release, which I granted and she ran on ahead just like the first time we met. A shrill whistle stopped her like a trained gun dog but she just stood awaiting further instruction. Clapping my hands and calling her name worked just fine as she bounded back then shot off in front again.

The River Eden crossing the moor

The river eroded the peat well below the moorland surface revealing a sandy gritty bed of stones and boulders. The tracks continued down the short steep bank at an angle to a crossing point marked with boulders set in two lines across the river. It was a little too deep for my boots so a short diversion was required. In my excitement, I forgot to visit the mobile phone rock but there was time on the return journey, and I was not relishing a shower of meaningless emails.

I was now high on the far bank I had seen from the beach and on reaching the ridge, the Atlantic and the Summer Isles lay before me. The bothy was an ideal lookout for spy trawlers or incoming unfriendly visitors. We were rather paranoid in those days, a feeling reignited by President Putin. A side door gave access to the cabin. A simple stone construction dug into the moorland and the exposed stonework and roof covered in an insulating and disguising layer of living heather sods, like a grouse butt. The front had a large single pane window protected by a shutter, hinging upwards and held aloft by wooden posts. All the woodwork had been green, probably army olive drab, but now weathered away to an attractive silver grey.

A simple wooden bench sat in front of a full width counter probably for charts, record books and the observers' elbows, holding their binoculars gazing westward. After a contemplative rest, Jessie and I set off for our appointment with the internet. We crossed the river after I had explored a few of the pools downstream confirming my view that fish could migrate to the redds and perhaps a loch or lochan above.

Mobile Rock

Returning to the track and then diverting to my right I could see Paradise Beach below and the fingers of stone where I first saw Penny leaving the water. In front, was the large round outcrop nicknamed mobile rock, so taking my mobile from its pouch on my belt I switched on and started waving in search of an elusive hint of a signal. Nothing at first, so I clambered up the rock and, wonder of wonders, a volley of emails pinged at me like a machine gun. I spent the next half hour unsubscribing from as many as possible, deleting spam ladies wanting to have a good time with me. Who needed them? I was having the time of my life! I did respond to several family members assuring them that

I was fine but communication was difficult. Having assuaged my guilt, I switched off before they had a chance to reply or heaven forbid call me. In any case, Jessie was eager to return to the Croft.

After my cheese and damson pickle sandwich, I spent the afternoon exploring the cottage. I felt like an intruder, a burglar, searching for something to steal, not cash or jewellery but something more valuable, information, an insight, a clearer deeper grasp of what makes Penny tick. What is life really like here? After all I have only been here a couple of days, and I have slept with a beautiful woman I saw walking naked out of the sea. This is the stuff of dreams, of fantasy. I pinched myself hard on my forearm to establish I was not dreaming. I dare not call on my search skills learned as a detective so many years ago. It would be an outrage, an invasion of privacy and trust to turn out drawers and cupboards so I confined my search to a purely visual one. I turned the pages of a few of the celebrity books to see words of appreciation to Penny the editor.

I examined her paintings, skilfully capturing the changing light and the sea most effectively. I was impressed. One in particular made me take a second glance. I had missed it last night and again today as I scanned past it. It was our beach, bright sun, the rocky fingers of the changing rooms and a small naked figure with long blonde hair walking out to sea. Whilst the other paintings were moody and atmospheric, this painting shone out reflecting her idea of paradise, naked and free, at one with nature. It was entitled Tràigh Pàrras.

Wandering round outside, I found her flotsam and jetsam corner at the side of the Croft, a pile of driftwood, lengths of plain and coloured rope, cork floats from fishing nets, orange plastic buoys and boat fenders. Scallop and razor clam shells grabbed my attention for future foraging missions.

It was time to transform myself into a knowledgeable sommelier and waiter, but also to present myself to Penny's friends in a favourable light. Did they know of my sudden arrival in her bed? What would they think of Penny? Then a sudden thought; 'was I the latest of many men?' There was only one way to find out. Donning my tweed trousers, pink shirt, a blue tie dotted with matching pink spots and my freshly polished brogues I was ready to join the fray.

Anja purred through the gears climbing the glen road and reducing to a steady idle on the plateau beyond. We stopped briefly taking in the sights, the mixed woodland lining the burn up to the moor above and the lochan beyond that merited a future fishing expedition. To the left we encountered another lochan, the source of the river and on both sides a line of grouse butts newly refurbished for the coming season. There could be work here for me as a loader on shoot days, beating was a bit too much for my knees wading through the deep springy heather.

Gàradh Eden Lodge loomed up in front. Two large stone pillars formed an entrance carrying a painted nameplate. It was a simple building built for a purpose rather than impressing visitors and neighbours. To have a lodge on a grouse moor with salmon fishing was evidence enough of one's wealth without the need for architectural frills. Three stories rendered with a creamy white paint and topped with a slate roof and tall terracotta chimney pots. The sash windows were all of an equal size, the upper lights being arched dormers set into the roof. The main entrance was a large oak door set in a square tower with a four-sided tented roof. The stone chip drive lead to a large forecourt so Anja crunched around to find the servants' car park.

Gàradh Eden Lodge

Following the aroma of food cooking, I found the single story kitchen at the end of the main house. I wondered what Penny had told them, how would I be perceived, and introduced to the staff? I would have to play by it ear and follow her lead. With a deep breath and drawing, myself up, I turned the handle and strode purposefully into the kitchen. As you would expect I brought everything to a silent standstill, apart from Penny striding over to plonk a warm kiss on my cheek. "This is Charles everybody."

I waved a "Hello everyone." to Sue who was head cook, Isla and Charlotte a part time teenage maid and waitress. She seemed the least interested returning to her Iphone.

"Come on in Charles. Delighted you can help because we are up to our necks." Sue welcomed, walking over to shake my hand. Isla waved and I recognised Morag who embraced me warmly thanking me for the fish. So far so good.

Sue instructed, "Penny will show you the wine and the menu.

The tables are set. They have wine glasses and the important thing is the welcoming drink of fizz, water or orange juice."

"Leave it with me I am sure I can deal with that."

Penny took me to the dining room, quite baronial with pitch pine beams and wooden panelling. Family portraits of austere looking Victorians adorned the walls alongside numerous stags' heads, a perfect example of Scottish hospitality, complete with a roaring fire fed from a huge wicker basket on wheels, full of logs. A green leather and ornate brass fender completed the ensemble and I could imagine the laird returning from a shoot, cold and wet, to sit there and warm himself with a tot of whisky.

The long mahogany table bedecked with silver sculptures of red deer, leaping salmon, pheasant and grouse added to the sporting theme. Penny directed me to a serving counter across the end of the room, bearing Champagne flutes set, ready for filling, on a silver salver and the fridge stocked with the fizz,

"Prosecco, I'm afraid." moaned Penny... "Orange juice there and buckets of ice. For the table, red or white, Merlot or Chardonnay. Don't leave the bottles on the table just keep circulating and filling up. Shout if you need anything." and she was off to the kitchen.

Having checked I knew where everything was, especially the corkscrew, one of those pump up ones that made uncorking less of a tug of war. I was fine with fizz bottles as I had my own system; remove foil, twist the wire cage six times but leave it on the cork, holding the bottom of the bottle against your abdomen grip the cork and twist the bottle. Looks like you know what you are doing and no one gets a flying cork in their soup.

Gàradh Eden Lodge

The ground floor was a series of lounges, one with a small bar that Sue and her husband David would work after dinner. Various doors led to toilets, cloakrooms, a boot room, a gunroom where guests could chain their guns to wooden dockets on the wall above a seat, rather like a golf club changing room. A grand staircase swept up to a stained glass window on the first landing and, like the ground floor, festooned in stags' heads, stuffed fish and game birds. Running along one side of the house is the ballroom, now a wedding and function venue. Huge mirrors at each end gave the illusion of a never-ending room.

Gàradh Eden Lodge ballroom

The main corridor displayed several paintings by Penny and some extremely attractive beachcomber art; I suppose you would call it. One in particular, a sea horse made from small pieces of shell, and scallop shells painted with gold edges and an underwater scene of a sea horse. My admiration for her talent was growing, overflowing even.

The sounding of a horn summoned everyone to the front door as a small coach rolled to a halt, its passengers eagerly viewing their accommodation through steamy windows. Sue extended a welcome as the driver unloaded the cases, nodding at me to carry them inside. The paint boxes and easels would remain in the coach until tomorrow. Sue took a roll call issuing room keys and directions, with an invitation for an aperitif at 6pm, an hour away.

Sue asked me to sound the dinner gong at the bottom of the stairs and I soon had it reverberating through the house, calling the artists to the dining room for their glass of fizz. Penny was on hand, attired in her black cocktail dress to conduct artistic small talk with the guests. She smiled and nodded at me reassuring that all was going well as I circulated topping up their glasses. Several asked if I was the laird but the mischievous old gentleman was kept under strict lock and key.

Happy hour passed quickly and convivially and I was on my starting blocks ready to step forward with wine for the table. Most took white wine with their Cullen Skink and Merlot with their venison casserole. I continued my duties until they rose to sit in the lounge by the roaring log fire. It was time to help clear and reset for breakfast. Fortunately, the kitchen had a catering dishwasher so about nine Penny and I were sent home with great appreciation. Penny unpacked a basket with two plated dinners and half a bottle of wine. Exhausted by our return to a working life we were keen to hit the sack. By the time I climbed into bed, Penny was fast asleep and I lay there briefly just looking at her.

The next morning Penny drove to the lodge to start her art classes. My role was to walk Jessie and meet for a picnic lunch near mobile rock. I arrived as the coach driver was unloading the paint boxes, canvases and easels so I was press-ganged once more. Sue followed with hampers and helped with drinks. Penny was in her element going from easel to easel commenting and advising as they painted our beach and the Summer Isles.

By 3pm, my work was done, so Jessie and I retreated to the Croft for a quiet pot of tea where I set up my fishing tackle. Saturday evening was a Ceilidh for the guests but twelve dancers do not a Ceilidh make, so favoured locals were recruited to make the night go with a swing. The ballroom was now a dance hall with tables round the edge. Davy ran the bar and Sue, Isla and Charlotte prepared a running buffet. Penny returned to the Croft to freshen up and change into her white blouse and tartan pleated skirt.

"I'm afraid I don't have a kilt Penny. I remember plaguing mother for one when we were on holiday in Edinburgh and I have an American friend who has several."
"You will be fine in slacks and open neck shirt." she smiled.

Anja got all three of us to the lodge in time for the buffet, a table groaning with rare beef, hot roast sides of salmon, venison pasties, numerous salads and dressings. It must take a lot of advance planning to get all this together out here. I helped with wine and Penny served the buffet while Sue and Isla took a well-earned breather. The band was tuning up in the ballroom as the local guests arrived, all paying a nominal fee for the privilege. The caller was an expert at getting people with three left feet dancing, even myself, and soon we were all wheeling, reeling, whooping and hollering. Even the eighty-year-old retired gamekeeper was on his toes whirling and twirling the ladies.

Later in the evening, I found him in the lounge having a quiet moment by the fire. "Hello I'm Charles. I believe you are Mr Horcus?"
" Aye Joe. You can call me Joe. You are the new man from England I gather."
"Yes that's me."
"Stopping at the Croft are you?"
"Er, yes that's right."
Joe breathed a long drawn-out "Aye" with a knowing sigh and twinkle in his eye.
"You fish then. I hear you caught some Pollock."
"My goodness! News travels fast round here."
"Aye well very little happens here so anything new soon gets round."
"Jungle bagpipes I suppose."
"Aye, that's right. Jungle bagpipes. I like that."
"I gather you come from a long line of keepers Joe."
"My so many times great grandmother was Orcadian," he paused to see if I understood that she was from the Orkneys before continuing, "she married an Orkney man who went to Canada working for the Hudson Bay Company. They married when he had made a bit of money and moved to the mainland to manage an estate. His sons took up keepering and so my grandfather and

father were all keepers."
"Can I get you a malt Joe."
"Aye, Talisker would be good."
I noted he had a jug of water next to his glass for a wee suspicion, just a spot to suit his taste.

Joe extracted my sporting experiences of fishing and shooting including grouse and many years of loading. The more he extracted the more he warmed to me.

"So this where you are. Chatting with Joe. It will soon be the last dance and Auld Lang Syne." Penny chided.

I shrugged my shoulders and Joe nodded his understanding.
"I hope we can continue our chat Joe?"
"Aye, I will look forward to that. Call at the house anytime."

"Well you have certainly made an impact there; invites from Joe are a rare privilege." admired Penny.

I relished the thought of the last waltz with her but after Auld Lang Syne the band started to pack up and the dancers drifted away. Instead of dancing cheek to cheek, we were waltzing pots and glasses to the kitchen, but many hands made light work of clearing up. Once again, we were too tired to do anything but sleep.

> Charles would waltz with a strawberry blonde
> And the band played on
> He'd glide cross the floor with the girl he adored
> And the band played on
>
> His brain was so loaded
> It nearly exploded
> The poor girl would shake with alarm
> He'd ne'er leave the girl with the strawberry curls
> And the band played on

SOUL SEARCHING AND SEA TROUT

It was Groundhog Day as Penny delivered my morning mug of tea. She was off for a post breakfast question and answer session before leading a walk over the moor to sketch Alex restoring a grouse butt with the seascape in the background.

I had yet to meet Alex so this was an ideal opportunity to make myself known. Moorland keepers by the very nature of their work, can be stubbornly insular individuals, working alone for days and weeks on end, in all weathers, counting chick hatches, fighting the elements, burning the heather, building butts and repairing washed out tracks. All for just a few days grouse shooting for the owner and his guests, fellow moor owners, shooting their moors in return. An excess of grouse affects the health of the birds causing populations to crash so keepers band together to reduce numbers to a sustainable level. Such invitations would be highly prized and hard, if not impossible to come by.

Alex was at the house greeting the guests dressed in his estate tweed, deerstalker, jacket and matching plus-fours hanging well down his legs over the top of his boots, explaining that the overlap keeps out rain and dirt from the heather. He looked the part, lean and powerful.

Armed with sketchbooks, the party mounted a trailer drawn by tractor and set off across the moor to the lochan behind Penny's croft. The lochan sat in a bowl well below the level of the moorland draining into the burn past the cottage. The ground rose steeply around the sides of the lochan with an almost sheer wall of rock at the far end, a mare's tail of a waterfall dropping into the rocks on the edge of the lochan, fed by a burn and a bigger, more distant, lochan beyond. It was picturesque given the light and reflections on the water. A line of heather grouse butts ran from the lochan, the last of which and nearest the water, was the latest to be restored.

In a scene like Mellors from Lady Chatterley's Lover Alex removed his jacket rolling his shirt sleeves over his muscled arms to dig heather sods and layer them on the butt. Penny gave some pointers as the guests pencilled their sketches. Periodically Alex would pause leaning on his spade and pose gazing into the distance with a striking profile. He knew the part he had to play and played it well.

Penny unpacked the picnic lunch that I helped to distribute, ensuring Alex was supplied with food and beer. It was obvious from his conversation that he had spoken at length with Joe, gently interrogating me to satisfy his curiosity and my expertise as a shooter and a loader. I think I passed the examination but decided not to offer my services at this early stage.

Lunch over; we moved back to the Lodge, for an exercise, picking out a feature to focus on, an old wooden gatepost, dry-stone wall, the wind-blown thorn trees, a line of silver birch etc. I left them to it walking Jessie back to the croft. Penny would stay and conduct a question and answer and commentary session on their work.

I lit a fire and read one of the celebrity books with little interest until I heard the latch click. Morag had dropped her off and Penny was obviously drained. Again, we had plated meals from the lodge. Making her sit by the fire, I put her feet on a footstool while I sorted the food and a glass of wine. She was most grateful.

"I only have to see them off in the morning. They will be gone by nine thirty and the rest of the day is ours. What shall we do?"

"Oh, walk, swim, fish?" I proffered.

"Sounds good. Any more wine?"

The next morning I was first up as Penny slept on. I heard the toilet flush and she appeared in her silk dressing gown in need of a mug of tea. Having collected eggs from the hens, I was able to offer scrambled eggs on toast for breakfast.

"There is some salmon left over from the lodge we can have with it."

Showered and hair dried she was back to perfection.

After waving goodbye to her artists, we enjoyed a slow start to the day with coffee in the morning sun.

"I wonder what the rest of the world is doing today?" posed Penny.

"You can bet they won't be at peace with the world or each other." I replied from under my sunhat perched forward of my eyes as I bathed in the warmth of the early morning sun.

"When it warms up we could go for a swim. Have we anything we need to do here?"

"I suppose I could tidy and water the garden. We need some logs for the basket."

Coffee concluded, Penny went to her garden, showing me the contents of her poly tunnel.

"I got the inspiration from Gardeners World, a couple on the Knoydart Peninsula were growing all sorts in their garden and tunnel, even melons, so I thought I would give it a go."

So far, I had not discussed my literary attempts with Penny given her expertise as a publisher so made no mention of my visit to Inverie en route. Instead, I complimented her green fingers and headed for the axe stuck in a chopping block, proceeding to split a pile of logs and transfer a load to the basket by the fire. The rest I stashed under the log store lean-to against the house.

"Who was it who said 'man who cuts wood for the fire is warmed twice'? He was right. Especially in this sun!"

"Or was it 'only mad dogs and an Englishman cut logs in the noon day sun?" chortled Penny. "Lemonade?"

"How about a picnic and swim."

I didn't bother to extricate my swimming shorts so grabbing towels, we strolled past the jetty and on to the white sands as the tide was receding. The fingers of rock were now a hotspot sheltering us from the breeze and providing a little shade. I made the water first with Jessie at my heel. Penny followed, sauntering model-like before a short sprint and launching herself into the sea with a dive, swimming about thirty yards before turning and waving for me to join her. The water was just reaching her shoulders and, as I swam to her, she grabbed my arms in an embrace and a salty kiss. I could tell this was going to be a good day.

The shallow water gave me an opportunity to survey the seabed looking for signs of life, hopefully a few scallops. Sure enough, I disturbed one. The gritty, sandy surface provided the ideal speckled habitat and camouflage for scallops settling into the substrate. If disturbed, they clap their shells shooting away on a jet of water. Moving into deeper water floating face down I thought I could see the raised shells protruding as a slight mound but at five metres down they were beyond my reach. Penny was floating basking in the sun when I drew alongside.

"Penny for them Penny."

"I don't have any thoughts, nor a care in the world at the moment. I am at peace with myself. I saw a poster once of a woman swimming into the sunset with the caption, 'Into The Water I Go To Lose My Mind and Find my Soul' I believe it a misquotation from John Muir."

I was now basking alongside gazing into our blue heaven until a barking Jessie shattered our piece returning us to vertical and quickly covering our nakedness, but the beach was deserted. Time for lunch.

I told Penny about the scallop bed but we would need snorkelling gear and a wetsuit to reach them. That would probably mean a trip to Inverness putting the idea on the back burner. The tide was at its full ebb revealing the maximum expanse of beach. Time to explore.

Penny sunbathed, but my pink and pasty skin would burn in the piercing rays of light and heat so covering up, I headed to the water's edge. Coiled worm casts indicated the tail ends of lugworm burrows, adjacent to a small depression being the mouth end of the U shaped tunnel. Good fishing bait if you have a spade, energy and a sound back. Three nil to the lugworm on this occasion.

Of greater interest were key-shaped holes home to the razor clam. All I need to extract the long shell and its tasty contents was a bottle of table salt. One nil to the razor clam but I now knew where they live. I'll be back!

Walking the water's edge, I eventually came to a deeper channel cut into the bed by the current from the river. It was several feet deep and I did my best to chart its course with landmarks for a future fishing foray, this evening perhaps.

My return journey took me along the high water mark beachcombing for anything artistic. I was a child again, exploring the large expanse of recently submerged pools in the margin where sea consumed the grassy bank at high tide. Ruby red anemones waved their tentacles at me, tiny brown shrimp skittered hither and thither, a Mermaids Purse, shells, peeler crab, various seaweeds and tiny fish.

Returning to Penny I lay by her side, she on her back and myself on my front looking at her profile.

"Have you found your soul?"

Penny was slow to respond. "Can one ever know what a soul is or whether it is possible to recognise it? I have frequently researched a definition of one's soul, something spiritual, an immaterial part of a human being or animal, regarded as immortal. Some say that death is just one-step in a soul's journey through the universe. Others, an emotional or intellectual energy or intensity, especially as revealed in a work of art or an artistic performance."

It was my turn for a slow response as I had to ponder her words and remained silent thinking more was to follow.

"Have I found my soul? Well I am at peace with the world.

Content with my lot. I have a safe home in wondrous surroundings, the sea, the beach, mountains, my faithful Jessie, money in the bank and food in the larder. I survived Covid. I am in good health. I have helpful and caring friends. I suppose all these things really amount to a state of happiness or contentment. I realise and appreciate I am extremely fortunate. What more do I need?"

I hoped the list might have included me but perhaps I came under helping caring friends.

"I think I verge on my soul being emotional or intellectual energy that is expressed in my painting." she philosophised.

"Does the painting of the naked woman on the beach represent a finding of your soul emerging from your other ethereal perhaps soulful pictures?"

That was rather deep for my intellect and was not sure if I even understood what I had said and waited for a response. Eventually Penny rolled on her side draping an arm and a leg over my prostrate body.

"Quite possibly." she whispered in my ear, licking the edge of my ear lobe followed by a touching of lips on my cheek "Shall we go to bed?"

If this were a scene from the Hollywood blockbuster, From Here to Eternity, we would be rolling in the waves, pounded by the surf, to soaring orgiastic orchestral strings, the thunder of the waves, trembling bodies, the look of intent in our eyes. All well and good for Burt Lancaster and Deborah Kerr, but sand does not mix well with moving parts in lovemaking.

"Are you going fishing tonight?"

"I thought I might try for a sea trout at high tide. Do you want to come?"

"No. I have an idea about a painting so I want to try some sketches."

"A seascape?"

"Not quite." she responded being rather mysterious.

"There is a gap in the line of paintings on the wall and I have been seeking inspiration for a painting to fill it."

Scanning the wall, I noted the portrait of her parents followed by a line of her soulful, ethereal works with darker, foreboding skies, followed by a gap and the naked swimmer on the sun-kissed beach. What, if anything, should I read into the way the paintings were displayed? I am no art expert and my only interpretation may be the gloomy skies expressing her grief for her parents. Then something changed her life lifting the gloom and letting in the sun. Hark at me waxing lyrical!

"See you later then. It may be dark when I get back."

My thoughts changed to fishing, something I had not done since my day of arrival. I reached my landmark as the light was fading, the sun hiding in the clouds about to descend behind the promontory on the far side of the estuary. I had my Hardy ten-foot fly rod and a smaller spinning rod, both set up ready to fish.

On the fly rod, I had a team of three flies, two single hooked Black Pennel, Bloody Butcher and on the point or end a larger, heavier wee double, Teal, Blue and Silver to carry my flies down quickly into the deep channel.

I recalled a poem by John Gray from his excellent book Sea Trout Nights.

> Home from the sea the rapid run
>
> Home to the redd the journey done
>
> To lie and wait by light of day
>
> To stir and wake as green turns grey

I started my first cast standing on the edge of the beach where the river entered the sea. The tide colliding with the flowing river causing a bubbling and boiling as each fought for supremacy over the other. The channel I had reconnoitred earlier was probably nine or ten feet deep now and my plan was to cast across the flow at a forty five degree angle where the line would be caught by the current and dragged in a sweep across the pool into slack water at the dangle.

The art is to keep the line straight and moving slowly. A bow drags the flies too quickly as they accelerate and climb toward the surface, but a deft flick of the rod tip mends or throws the bend upstream slowing the line and allowing the flies to seek their prey.

John Buchan said; "The charm of fishing is that it is the pursuit of what is elusive but attainable, a perpetual series of occasions for hope. Any hour may bring to the most humble practitioner the capture of the monster of his dreams. But, with hope goes regret, and the more ardent the expectations of the fisherman, the bitterer will be the sense of loss when achievement fails him by the breadth of the finest hair. It is a bitterness which is commonly soon forgotten, for the same chance may occur tomorrow or next week."

A pace forward follows every cast, gradually covering the pool in a series of sweeps. Every cast is full of hope and expectation anticipating a delicate pluck of the fly, firing adrenaline into your bloodstream ready to strike. No Luck. Cast again feeling for the lightest touch, a loud unseen splosh in the dark as a restless sea trout leaps from the water. The fish are here. Cast again. A pluck and then a grab! Quickly now lift the rod. Pull in the slack line. Give no quarter for the fish will leap and twist to throw your fly back at you. Keep the line tight but let it run as the fish pulls away back to the sea. Slow his progress with tension on the line until he stops and turns. Hope your knots do not fail. Now pull in that slack as the fish runs back at you, ready to leap once more. The sea trout fresh from the sea is fit and strong but eventually will tire and come towards your net. Careful now as many fish have a last gasp at the net, so push the net down in the water, right arm holding the rod high, left arm slipping the net under the fish and deftly scooping up your prize.

It is a good fish of about three pounds and worthy of keeping for the eating. Sea trout gather in shoals especially at the mouth of the river waiting for the right conditions to run upstream. Taking note of where I hooked the fish I continued with my task until I had covered the channel as far as I could reach and as far as I dare wade.

Sea Trout

The tide was on the turn and it was time for me to ebb back to Penny triumphant with my prize. Jessie signalled my arrival and I saw some hurried activity through the window as Penny tidied her sketchings.

"Any luck?"

"A lovely sea trout." I beamed holding the fish for her to see.

Penny took the fish while I returned my rods to the store and removed my waders.

"I think that deserves a damson gin." She proclaimed.

"A cup of tea would go down well."

All in all, a day, and a fish to remember.

KILT AND HAGGIS

Penny answered the telephone. It was Sue from the lodge and there then followed a slightly guarded conversation raising my suspicion that something was amiss. Penny kept the details to herself but after breakfast stated she just had to pop up to the lodge and see Sue. No reason was given, nor requested by myself dismissing the call as something ladies needed to discuss alone.

Penny seemed uneasy and pensive on her return, again not willing to reveal anything. I offered a concerned, "Everything ok?" with an unconvincing response of "Yes fine."

I chopped a pile of logs and stocked the fireside basket. Lunch was a quiet affair involving small talk about the weather and other trivial subjects. Something was afoot and I had not seen Penny like this.

Taking a mug of tea to the garden, I changed the nylon cast on my sea trout rod, checked the barbs, often blunted or snapped off when in contact with stones, and then retying the flies to a new cast. All was ready for an evening trip to the river mouth pool. Perhaps Penny would join me or maybe continue her sketching.

"Charles. Can you come in a minute?" She called whilst curling her index finger in a slightly suggestive manner. Penny had my full attention and I followed her in.

"In the bedroom." she instructed.

"Drop your trousers!"

Things were getting interested.

"Don't get all excited, you can put that away! No time for that!"

Whereupon she held a bath towel in front of me before wrapping it round my waist.

"Hold it please!" And took a couple of paces back.

My face must have been a picture of confusion and

bewilderment.

"I want to see what you might look like in a kilt."

"What would I want with a kilt? I'm a Sassenach. How can I wear a kilt?

"They've asked at the lodge if you would wear a kilt for an event."

Now the object of the phone call was becoming clear.

Before I could splutter an 'Och aye' or 'Och nae', I was pushed in the chest falling backwards onto the bed, followed by Penny lying on top of me and smothering any chance of a verbal response with a long sloppy passionate kiss.

Lying on the bed, side by side, recovering from our exertions I observed,

"I think I would have said yes to the kilt without resorting to the use of such persuasive powers. After all, my grandfather served with the Royal Scots in India, and WW1 wearing tartan trews and guarded Edinburgh Castle. My sister lives in Scotland and her daughter married a Scot, so I must be able to claim political asylum or domiciliary status. Surely I can claim to be an honorary Scot."

"Oh the persuasive power was nothing to do with the kilt!" Penny laughed leaping out of bed, grabbing her dressing gown and heading for the door.

"They want you to host a Burns evening and recite the address to the haggis. I will make tea."

"Whaaaat?"

The tea tray edged round the door testing if it was safe to enter, followed by Penny peeping round the jamb with a mischievous smile.

"What about Alex, Angus or Davy doing it."

"All the men are at the Highland Show."

"Looks like a done deal then. No further persuasion needed."

"Sue will be so pleased and grateful."

"I will need some time to learn the address. It's not the easiest bit of prose for a Scot never mind a pseudo one. When is it?"

Once again, Penny leapt from the bed, "Saturday evening."

"Whaaat?"

Sacrificing my evening sea trout fishing, Penny and I walked Jessie to mobile rock to Google 'Address to a haggis' in written and spoken form. We both struggled with pronunciation so I proposed seeking Joe's help as he spoke Gaelic. He was happy to help although he was somewhat amused at the prospect of a posh Sassenach getting his tongue round Burns' most famous work.

It was midsummer so a Burns supper traditionally held on Burns Night the 25th January, was unheard of. The event was a late booking for a party of Americans on a flying whirlwind tour of Scotland and would be at the lodge for one night only.

The Prince Charlie outfit is a style of jacket and kilt traditionally worn with ghillie brogues, a full-dress sporran, and a bow tie. It belonged to one of the past members of the lodge family and smelled of mothballs so Penny hung it in the breeze to freshen it up. "Splash a bit of Old Spice on it." she recommended.

"Come on! Get your kit off!" she jested, "and your kilt on."

"Well. Well. Don't you look the business? You are a bonnie prince. Very sexy." She purred slinking over to me, draping her arms around my shoulders and plonking a kiss on my cheek. My attempted embrace was immediately repulsed.

"Not that sexy. Well, not now anyway. Get your kilt off and hang it up."

My background as a trainer gave me the confidence to perform the address but I also wanted to make the whole evening a memorable event with a bit of theatre. Charlotte the quiet young kitchen maid was also in the local pipe band and agreed to help with a performance on the bagpipes. As the coach arrived, she played a rousing Scotland the Brave welcome as I greeted them from the coach.

Following drinks in the ballroom, Sue led a tour of the lodge identifying the family ancestors in the portraits. The ladies had begged, stolen and borrowed anything to do with Burns including a reasonable framed picture, the Saltire and US flags.

Robert Burns, 1759 – 1796

I chose one female visitor to sound the gong, which she did with great gusto, repeatedly. Charlotte piped them to their seats with the national anthem Flower of Scotland. The nations' flags on poles stood at the end of the mantelpiece, the log fire blazing beneath. Sue, Penny, Isla, Morag and Charlotte stood in line ready to serve and pipe, resplendent in tartan skirts and white blouses.

"Ladies and gentlemen. May I extend to you the warmest of welcomes to Gàradh Eden Lodge. And trust that you will enjoy the best of traditional Scottish hospitality on our Burns Night supper.

"Will you please be upstanding for your national anthem."

Penny hit the button on the CD player and the Star Spangled Banner reverberated round the rafters, sung with great gusto, hand on heart by our American cousins, followed by applause.

Ladies and gentlemen please remain standing for the Selkirk Grace."

"Some hae meat and canna eat,

And some wad eat that want it,

But we hae meat and we can eat,

And sae the Lord be thankit."

"Our first course is Cock-a-leekie soup, a Scottish dish consisting of leeks and peppered chicken stock, often thickened with barley. The original recipe added prunes during cooking, and as traditionalists, we still garnish our version with a julienne of prunes.

Ladies and gentlemen the Cock-a-leekie soup course."

Sue and Penny entered carrying a huge antique Ironstone ceramic tureen.

The diners, whipped to a minor frenzy, clapped heartily with excitement.

So far, so good. I kept the wine flowing, anticipating the obvious question about my underwear and an occasional surreptitious attempt to lift my kilt.

As the soup dishes were cleared, the butterflies were fluttering in my stomach.

"Ladies and gentlemen. America and the United Kingdom have enjoyed a long and special relationship, but it is often said we are two nations divided by the same language. For example,

Pants and trousers

Elevator and lift

Sidewalk and pavement

Garbage / rubbish

sweater / jumper

cookie / biscuit

french fries / chips

You get my drift. Burns' address to the haggis is a complicated work that many Scots have difficulty understanding, so I have prepared an English translation for you to read while I orate Burns' original words."

"And now, and now," I paused, waiting for complete silence, holding my hands in the air.

"And now ladies and gentlemen Burns Address to the Haggis."

Charlotte pumped up the bagpipes and Sue and Penny entered with two large steaming timorous beasties on silver salvers, marching round the table to the chanter of Charlotte's pipes, the diners clapping whooping and hollering. It is little wonder that people believe stories about hunting Haggis on the moors especially when served on a bed of flowering heather.

Sue and Penny placed the salvers in front of me between two

sgian-dubh, the ornamental knife traditionally worn in the top of the kilt hose. Beside each, a dram of malt whisky.

I paused.....until one could hear a pin drop.

"Fair fa' your honest, sonsie face,
Great Chieftain o' the Puddin-race!
Aboon them a' ye tak your place,
Painch, tripe, or thairm:
Weel are ye wordy of a *grace*
As lang's my arm."

Gentle reader, for brevity I have included the address in full at the end of the book together with the English translation.

I was in full flow, building to a crescendo. Grabbing a Sgean-dubh in each hand and raising them high, I was at fever pitch, bringing them down with great theatrical effect to pierce and slash the Haggis spilling the tasty gore within.

"His knife see Rustic-labour dight,
An' cut ye up wi' ready slight,
Trenching your gushing entrails bright,
Like onie ditch;
And then, O what a glorious sight,
Warm-reekin, rich!"

Raising a haggis in triumph to deliver the final line "Gie her a haggis!" was greeted with rapturous applause as their mobiles recorded my dramatic presentation for posterity and the folks back hame.

With a dram in each hand, I applied the whisky sauce and, raising my glass, "Ladies and gentlemen please join me in a toast to The Haggis."

Sue and Penny nipped in taking the Haggis to serve, while Charlotte, now pipe less, delivered the traditional accompaniments, bashed neeps, turnips and swede, and mashed tatties.

I thought some audience participation may help the evening

along so handed a copy of the address to the first diner at my side, asking her to read the first line and pass it on round the table. It was hilarious and great fun.

Sweet was Cranachan, followed by a cheeseboard and a chance to sample some of the single malts on offer.

Finally, we rounded off with Auld Lang Syne. Naturally they all wanted group and individual pix with their Bonnie Prince which I was happy to oblige. I caught Penny's eye several times who responded with a smile and a discreet thumbs up.

Charlotte turned out to be a talented musician. I had misjudged her as a teenager glued to her Iphone playing games or texting her boyfriend, but she came up trumps with a playlist of Ballade Pour Adeline, Glasgow Love Theme and other gentle songs to woo the weary tourists. Their early start to the day, one of many on their non-stop tour of Scotland in seven days, was beginning to tell. Hastened by some gentle music from the CD they filed out and off to bed.

The adrenalin buzz had also taken its toll on me as the worry of the last couple of days merged with weariness, food and alcohol. Penny drove me home and was rather quiet until we entered the cottage and she helped me remove my stage outfit. This time there was no "Get your kit off." Instead she purred "You were just magnificent. Wonderful. They loved you. We loved you. I loved you."

I was back at the lodge to oversee breakfast. The coach driver was in the hall loading a pile of cases in to the coach as I arrived. The tour guide was most complimentary about the evening and my performance. "The ladies, in particular, enjoyed it immensely." she winked.

I toured the table at breakfast wishing them God speed on their journey and a resounding "Haste ye back." Whereupon they filed out, all thanking me individually, slipping banknotes in to my hand. We waved them off into the sunrise breathing a sigh of relief that all had gone well, then returning to the kitchen for a coffee with the ladies to share my pocketful of tips.

Charlotte produced her Iphone for a full reprise of the dinner and my inaugural tour de force as the Bonnie Prince. "Sue and the boys wanted to see what they missed. See how you went on." she laughed.

"Well I hope they approve. I did my best as an honorary Scot."

"You did us proud. I sent the video to the owners last night. They are delighted and the tour company wants to make it a regular part of their itinerary."

Penny leaned on my shoulder and whispered, "See what you can do when you don't say 'No."

LOBSTER AND CRAB

Back at the croft Jessie was ready for a run so we walked the beach, paddled, sat, talked, threw stones for Jessie and just looked out to sea. Life here is so simple, so pleasurable. Strolling towards the river pool, I noticed something submerged a few yards out breaking the surface. At first, I thought it might be the head of a seal or even an otter but it did not move.

"Oh look it's a lobster pot." declared Penny. "That's a good find."

Sure enough, the pot was lodged in the sand in about two feet of water. Trousers off, I waded in tugging and rocking the pot until the sand released its grip. Towing it behind me, I managed but a few yards before the rope stopped me in my tracks. Returning to the water, I followed the rope as far as I could, pulling it out of the sand. Lo and behold, there was another pot, in deeper water, having dropped down the side of the channel. We both started a tug of war and finally the second pot started to slide towards us.

"What luck!" Penny cried out. "There's something in it."

Sure enough, the dark bluey-purple carapace of a lobster was waving its fingers at us.

"Lobster for tea? Or let him go?"

It was a good take-able size and no sign of it being a female carrying eggs on the underside.

Placing the pots side by side and standing between them, we picked them up one in each hand, myself at the front and Penny the rear. At the burn, Penny collected some rubber bands from the croft to manacle our catch, leaving him in the water, his pot firmly secured to the jetty.

I took the second pot to the garden for a closer examination. All looked well with all its bits intact and I was struck with the thought we could extend our diet beyond the excess of venison, good as it was, one can have too much of one thing. Penny had never cooked lobster and was squeamish about dealing with a living one.

"There are two ways to do it humanely, "I advised, based on my many years of watching TV chefs. "The point of a knife driven through the head or hold it in both hands and sharply twist the head off the body."

People can be very anthropomorphic and sentimental when dealing with living food. In times gone by grandparents kept pigs and chickens and slaughtering them was a necessity. Now we choose what bit we want wrapped in plastic, ignoring the fact that a slaughter man, now in a factory, had done our dirty work for us.

Penny pulled a face when I suggested twisting the head off and handed me a knife. The pan of boiling water was ready and she slipped the lobster in. Excellent fare.

I needed local knowledge about where, when and how to use our pots so Joe was the man to consult. He came out of his cottage eager to see the pots and to pat me on the back. "I've seen your video. You were very good. Better than some Scots I have seen. Let's look at these pots."

"I guess the trawlers have been in too close and ripped the pots out. It has happened a lot recently and the area is supposed to be a marine protection area."

Joe advised dropping them over the far side of the bay.

"Its all rocky there where the hill goes down steeply into the water. Good habitat for lobster and crab. Have you got a boat? It's a long drag over the top and hard walking. Easier in a boat straight across the bay."

This was a blow to my aspirations of being a lobster fisher and replied in the negative.

"The soldiers had one when they were at the croft. Must have taken it with them I suppose, along with the Landrover."

Joe then filled me in with details of their activities.

"They patrolled up down the glen road to the lodge and up the tracks on the moors checking on security though to be honest I never saw any threat. The lodge was all done up but I did not know until after that it was all for the Queen in an emergency. They used to come on my moor to a gulley where I tested my rifles. They didn't need any help, they were experts and good marksmen and they had machine guns. I had a go with one, it was good fun. They helped themselves to the deer so that was a bonus to the stalker. We carried on with the grouse and they would check the visitors out, Penny's father and guests from London, politicians, friends of the owners and so on. Other times they would be on their boat in the bay checking any boat that came near, or be in their hideout up yonder watching the western approaches. Must have been very boring really, but what a place to be bored in. Then one day we got notice the lodge was going back to the owners and they upped and left. The croft was locked up, as it belonged to the MOD, until Penny's father took it over. I have watched her grow from a young girl on holiday with her parents, nice people they were. It was good to see Penny back at the croft, living there for the last few years after her parents had passed on. Never seen a man there though, until you arrived."

If you let people talk, rather than interrogate them by bombarding with questions, you can discover many new lines of enquiry.

"How did you get on with Joe." Penny asked.

"Oh great. He has seen the video and was most complimentary. He told me where to try the pots on the far side of the bay but we need a boat to get them there. He says the soldiers had one."

"You mean Doris."

"Do I?"

"Yes Doris came with the Croft and we went out in her all the time. She is in the store out back next to the Landrover."

"You have a Landrover as well?" I exclaimed excitedly.

Penny opened a kitchen drawer and scrabbled about producing a key-labelled "Store."

Penny took me to the back of the Croft, unexplored territory for me. The rusty hinges creaked and groaned but finally opened to reveal shapes in the dark interior draped in tarpaulins. "I expect I will need my torch."

"Let there be light." Penny proclaimed flicking a bank of four light switches at the end of a metal conduit.

There was light indeed from four rows of hanging industrial lights.

"Give me a kiss because I may never see you again once you get ferreting in there."

"Of course you will darling. I will return for meals."

The first cover looked boat-like and the one beyond, the Landrover.

Sure enough Doris was woken from her slumbers, hidden beneath her canvas cover and mounted on a road trailer. Managing to drag her out into the sun for the first time in I don't know how many years, I was like a child on Christmas morning pulling a present from my sack. I had the presence of mind to take pix on my phone before a full revelation. The tarpaulins had done their job well keeping the dirt and bird droppings off her. She was clinker planked, probably mahogany, fastened with copper rivets to steam bent oak timbers.

Doris

Bronze lifting eyes in the keel indicated she could be lifted onto a jetty or more likely a mother ship when used as a tender.

The stem was laminated and probably a mahogany transom. The oak rubbing strake was fitted with a rope fender all round. A pair of oars could be used in two rowing positions on the oak gunwale. It was complete with a small anchor and warp line.

What a find. An absolutely fabulous little boat about ten feet long.

The all bronze fittings indicated a quality build and then I discovered a small bronze plaque declaring shipbuilding apprentices had built it for the Admiralty. The large bronze plaque on the transom clearly named this ship "Doris." A rather unimaginative unromantic name for a pretty little boat. I suppose Doris would have been appropriate if one's wife or daughter was called Doris but there was no-one in my family history of that name.

I digress with a small moan and rant. Standing there for a long time created the possibility that the clinkers may have shrunk and would let in water until rehydrated. Apart from a bit of cleaning and polishing, new rope work and some fenders she appeared ready to roll.

"Penny! Penny! Come and see what I have found. She's beautiful. Absolutely beautiful." She needs some fenders. Have you got any in your beachcombing pile?"

Penny stood silently, staring long and hard at her father's boat, running her hand gently along the gunwale and the oars as if feeling for his presence. I dare not speak for fear of interrupting or upsetting her contemplations, her memories.

"Yes she is beautiful. We had so many happy times in her, fishing....swimming.... exploring. Father loved her. Being in the boat on the loch was as far removed as he could get from his real life and work. It was his little bit of Heaven."

"She could be our bit of heaven Penny. She just needs tidying up, polish the bronze, some fenders and balers and some rope." I persuaded.

Penny took my hand putting my arm round her waist as we sauntered round to her flotsam and jetsam store piled outside a small shed. All the good stuff, useful things, are in there so be my guest. Several mixed fenders were soon released from custody and Penny produced some metal polish and rags. "See you at tea time."

When teatime arrived, I was summoned to the table with instructions to wash the dirt from my face and hair. "You need a pair of overalls." She observed. "How are we to get her down to the jetty, neither of us have tow bars and it is too steep for the two of us to manoeuvre?"

"I had not considered that part of my plan. I am still on page one making her beautiful and shipshape, just like you."

Rising to leave the tea table she ordered, "Not before the washing up, dried and put away, then you can play."

I wanted to say, "Oh Muuuuuuummmmm." but thought the better of it. Never in the field of human conflict has washing up been concluded so quickly to mis-quote Winston Churchill.

"Get off with you. I will bring coffee."

For the rest of the evening we worked on Doris and the trailer needing a little lubrication here and there. Even the winch and jockey wheel seemed ok. Penny was right about trying to manoeuvre it down to the jetty without a brake. "Do you think Angus at the farm could tow it down with his 4x4 or the quad?"

"I will ring him tomorrow. I'm sure he will oblige."

"Tomorrow?" I questioned disappointedly in my 'Oh Mummmmm' voice.

"It's nearly time for bed little man. You have a long day tomorrow. You need your sleep."

"Damson gin nightcap then."

Dawn could not come soon enough and Penny gave Angus time to finish milking. "Everything has its own time, and there is a specific time for every activity under heaven." Meaning his milking was more important than moving the boat. She was right of course. "Why don't we walk down and call in." I proposed. Jessie seemed to approve.

Once again, the sun smiled on us walking the loch edge, Jessie gambolling on the grass, as we held hands, sometimes my hand on her shoulder or her arm round my waist. The farm dogs heard us coming from a long way off, running to the farm gate but not beyond. Morag appeared and waved, welcoming us in.

"Angus has just finishing milking, he will be in for his breakfast shortly. Do you want a coffee?

"Sounds good, as long as we are not disturbing Angus."

Heavens, no! We don't get many visitors and he is always out on the farm.

Angus was a mountain of a man in every sense, height, width, girth, arms and legs like tree trunks. With a mass of curly reddish hair and full beard, he could easily be mistaken for one of his Highland Cattle. The kitchen went dark as Angus stood in the doorway blocking nearly all-available light.

"Angus. This is Charles. Penny's friend."

"Aye hello." He greeted offering a hand as big as a garden spade. I anticipated a bone-crunching grip but his hand was soft and gentle. "I've heard a lot about you, Charles and I've seen you on the video at the Burns supper."

"Here it comes." I thought, good or bad I have to take it.

"That took some courage to stand in front of those Yanks and recite Burns. I cuddna have done it. You were a natural and the tips were good eh Morag?"

"Well thank you Angus. It took a lot of persuading from Penny." I paused as Penny started to blush in fear that I might reveal the nature of that persuasion. But, I am a gentleman after all, "and I really enjoyed it. Great fun. How was the Highland show."

"Aye we had a good time. I took a Highland cow and calf to show and got a reserve champion so that's good for the herd. Alex came first in the tug o'war and I had a go in the amateur weight throw. It was great to catch up with farming friends, chew the fat, moan about the price of feed and all that and we had a wee drinkie as well."

"A wee drinkie! He was damn near unconscious when Alex dropped him in the farmyard. He spent the night in the barn covered up with a blanket."

It was Angus' time to blush but barely noticeable under all that red hair. He winked at me and smiled, then polished off a mammoth breakfast commenting, "Farmers need a lot of calories."

Weight Throw Highland Games

As we expected, Angus readily agreed to move the trailer giving us time to walk back before he set off. Angus slewed into the yard spinning the quad on a sixpence and expertly lining up the trailer. I have noticed that farmers do not tend to lift or move anything manually if it can be done by machine, which is why they become so expert at reversing and manoeuvring.

Towing it onto the road, he reversed into the track to the jetty, inching down the narrow slipway dipping Doris' stern in the water.

"I think you should launch her Penny."

Releasing the winch, Penny slipped our little boat into the water bobbing happily, as we watched for any signs of water seeping in. Angus disappeared in a cloud of blue smoke.

"I think she is happy to be on the water again. To be alive. To do what she was built for. It must have been awful shut up in the dark," observed Penny, her eyes misting over. I thought this could be an emotional moment for her so came equipped with a freshly laundered hankie to dab her eyes.

"You know Penny her presence has brought the whole jetty back to life, she has completed a picture of the loch, a missing piece in a jigsaw."

Hark at me waxing lyrical again, but restoring life to an inanimate object was an emotional moment for me as well. I fashioned a couple of balers out of plastic containers, cutting a corner off to make a scoop, and then tied on a length of cord to prevent loss overboard.

Every morning and throughout the day I would jog down to ensure she was still afloat. Water was seeping between the planks in places but not a lot to worry about and I left it to sink back into the wood. Finally all seemed to be bone dry with the bottom drying out.

As I planned our launch day over breakfast one Sunday morning, I was brought down to earth with a bump.

"Who will be rowing?" Penny enquired mischievously, tight-lipped and attempting to stop a smile breaking out all over her face. "An outboard motor would be useful."

I was lost for words. I was so besotted that I had not given a single thought to propulsion. There was no mast so it was oars or a motor. I was sitting with my elbows on the table my head in my hands, not knowing what to say or how to resolve the problem.

"Never mind darling we can get one some time and in the meantime we can share the rowing perhaps. I can show you how to go on; I always rowed for my father. I should have detected that Penny was being naughty and devious but I was desolate, in despair.

"Let's go and see if she is ok and perhaps have a trial row."

Unbeknown to Penny, I had renamed the boat using the best sign writing I could muster. We were ready for our maiden voyage but had no champagne to launch her into a new life of service on the sea. Neither did we want a broken glass bottle in the slipway. On the River Spey they bless the water with a bottle of Aberlour whisky to mark the beginning of the salmon season, so why not bless our boat with the same.

Taking my hand, she walked down the drive on to the lane. As we turned the corner towards the track, I thought I caught a glimpse of someone. Jessie ran off down the track and started barking. "She will be chasing the ducks, I expect" proffered Penny.

As we turned down the track, the drone of bagpipes was followed by cheers and clapping from all our friends on the jetty. A table was set with a basket of venison pasties, wine and whisky. Our dinghy floated happily by the pontoon but there was something different. Then I realised on the transom was a small outboard motor, a British made Seagull, a single cylinder water-cooled two-stroke engine, known as "The Best Outboard Motor for the World", renowned for their simplicity and reliability.

Seagull Outboard

I was speechless. Penny admonished me jovially with, "How could you think I was going to row you across that loch?"

"But where? Where is it from? How has it got here?"

"Better ask Joe."

"It was Penny's fathers' outboard and she found it wrapped up in the back of the garage. So we crept in while you were out and I have got it going again, all it needed was the points cleaning and some fresh two-stroke. She's as good as new."

I was still speechless, spluttering tearful thanks to Joe and hugging Penny.

"This is the launching party so let's have a drink and then you can play." advised Penny, "Better make a little speech."

"This a wonderful surprise to see all our friends here to share in our launch party. Many thanks to the ladies for the pasties and I hope you will have a drink with us. Special thanks to Joe for his technical expertise, I don't know how you managed to keep it all a secret. I also have a little surprise for Penny who loves this beach and the loch so much, so I am going to ask her to remove the cover."

It was now Penny's turn to be mystified but she did as requested lifting the maroon canvas from the stern to reveal, "bean an locha" painted on the gunwale.

"bean an locha. Must be Gaelic but what does it mean?"

"Why don't you ask Joe?"

"It means Lady of the Loch." He revealed to great sighs and expressions of approval from the audience.

"Penny, you are my Lady of the Loch." resulted in a long warm hug, wiping her tears on my shoulder.

Even more sighs and a few tears of joy from the ladies.

It was time to get stuck into the refreshments and I made a

beeline for Joe to get all the practical information I would need.

It was time for the official naming ceremony and maiden voyage so I called on Penny to do the honours.

"I name this dinghy bean an locha, may she take us on many adventures and bring us home safe and sound."

Joe stepped forward with a bottle of whisky whispering, "Just a wee suspicion. We can drink the rest."

"Come on Joe fire it up."

Joe wound the starting cord around the motor, tickled the carburettor and with a single pull she roared into life. Roared is probably an overstatement as Seagulls go about their task with a gentle phut phut delivering a steady powerful push through the water but in no way would it ever be used for water skiing.

We both had a turn around the harbour to cheers from the jetty, in particular from Penny jumping up and down and waving with excitement and fond memories.

"Do you want a trip round the loch Penny?"

My excitement was tempered by her response that we needed to attend to our guests and clear up the debris from the party. "This afternoon will be fine."

I dare not manage my childish droning response. "Oh! But Muuummmmmmm!" She was right.

Back at the croft we sorted the glasses and the bottles and I waited for Penny to fire the starting gun.

"Just nipping to the loo." She said returning in her long dress, the one she wore when I first met, "Got a towel in case I go for a swim. Come on then Captain Ahab!"

"I hardly think I am a maniacal captain of a whaling ship!"

"Ok. Captain Cook then, he was a great explorer."

"Well that's better, but he was killed in Hawaii trying to get his longboat back from the natives. I see myself more as a swashbuckling Cap'n Jack Sparrow."

"You won't be going to Hawaii Charles, and I think your swash is well and truly buckled." she laughed.

The Seagull fired up and I shouted "Let go for'ard." and Penny obliged. Phutting out of the harbour we were able to observe the hidden beach and mobile rock from a different perspective, over the kelp forest and on towards the river pool where I showed her the channel. I continued carefully around the promontory with Penny looking for any submerged rocks. All appeared clear if we stayed a few yards off shore. Joe was right that the hill continued its descent into the water.

At the end of the promontory, we turned to port circling back but with a terrific view of the Summer Isles. As we passed the stony fingers in the beach, Penny was standing in the front of the boat, the breeze streaming through her hair and billowing her dress.

Recalling the famous scene from the film, "You are not on Titanic you know." She turned and smiled. The sunlight pierced her dress silhouetting and revealing her shapely body. "I can see your knickers through that dress."

"No you can't! I'm not wearing any!" whereupon the dress dropped to the floor and she dived overboard. We circled each other as she laughed and waved at me, truly a free spirit in the water. Truly the lady of the loch where she could live her life with joy and fulfilment.

Throwing her a rope, I shouted, "I'll give you a tow back."

It was great fun as she rolled headfirst on her back, on her front, one hand on the rope the other arm or a leg in the air like a synchronised swimmer. She swam the last few yards to the jetty where I pulled her from the water draping her in a dry towel that developed into one of her long hugs. Her silence said it all.

Over dinner, we discussed practical uses of the boat, fishing, the lobster pots, naked synchronised swimming, picnics, exploration, perhaps a trip to the island in the bay. Fishing we could do any time, but the lobster pots needed fresh bait preferably an oily fish like herring or mackerel.

"Why don't you invite Joe to go fishing like he did with father and I can get some peace and quiet to do my painting."

Joe jumped at the chance and got Alex to drop him off with his rod and flask. Never underestimate an older person they have seen it, done it, and got the T shirt, often before you were born.

"You take her out Joe if you want."

Both rods were now tackled up with a long nylon cast and a variety of coloured feathered hooks terminating with a lead bomb.

Joe thought the best spot would be towards high water on the edge of the straight where fish would follow the coast. Fortunately, a new anchor line was long enough to reach the bottom and hold us steady in a moderate to slack current and little breeze.

The method is quite simple, chuck it overboard and let the lead bomb hit the bottom. Wind up a few feet, then lift, and lower the road causing the feathers to swim like small fish. Joe was the first to strike winding in and lifting the trace and wriggling fish over the side. With a deft expert flick of the wrist, the mackerel fell splashing and slapping into his bucket.

I had my first hit with two on at once and Joe remarked we might be getting into a shoal. Sure enough, we were pulling three or more at a time and our buckets were overflowing. We had more than enough bait for the lobster pots but some fish were destined for our cooking pots and our friends.

Penny had been watching for our return from Mobile Rock meeting us at the jetty and delighted with our success. Safely docked and covered, we hauled our catch to the Croft sorting the smaller fish for bait and the larger ones gutted and cleaned for the freezer and "give aways."

Joe summoned Alex to collect him taking the bulk of the "give aways" for people at the lodge. Penny strung fish through their gills and mouths in a colourful fan for Morag and Angus, pedalling off on her bicycle to keep them fresh, returning about an hour later with more new potatoes. Penny deserved a long warm embrace and heartfelt thanks followed by a pot of tea. We discussed several ideas for expeditions but the priority was to get the lobster pots baited and in place. First, we needed a garden cane with a flag.

"I can do the flag. I have some bright yellow material." Nipping off to cut a square and attach strips to tie it to the cane. The cane was available in the garden and I found a length of hefty metal chain to act as a keel and hold it upright in the water. A five litre plastic container became the float lashed to the cane with gaffer tape and cable ties. It wasn't pretty, just effective and would suffice until I observed something better in one of the local harbours. I took it down to the jetty experimenting with the rope attached and a length of chain until it was floating upright.

The next morning the mermaid and I set off with our two pots to the far side of the loch. We chose a spot where a bush was a prominent landmark on the shore and dropped our first pot overboard weighted with a brick and baited with the mackerel. Moving along the shore, we dropped the second cage tied to the first and a length of rope rising to the float. The tide was rising so we returned to the kelp forest in search of more Pollock. Safely anchored we lay back watching our floats bob up and down alongside the tips of the kelp. Could life be more idyllic? I do not believe so.

They say that females are better at catching fish and on this occasion, her luck was in, her three to my one. That was enough for dinner and the freezer.

Penny was looking through the store cupboards. "You have eaten a lot of food since you arrived here." She chided. "Just look at this shopping list!" lifting the note board from the wall. True of course. It was time for that dreaded event, the supermarket run.

"Tomorrow any good?" I offered.

"I need to ring round and see if the others need anything."

The A835 is a sixty plus mile snake wriggling around rivers, lochs and mountains finally crossing the Beauly Firth into Inverness. Here you will find all the high street names so take your choice, perhaps mixing it with a bit of Polish or Indian, if you have time and the inclination. Anja's rear seats were laid flat and covered in large cardboard boxes to accommodate all the shopping we had been asked to get. The first two trolleys were for us and Penny left me packing while she went in again. I was given lots of instructions of what to do and not to do, "Mind the yoghurt," etc but I followed my own routine of dairy stuff, fruit and veg, tinned, bottled, dry goods etc for ease of unpacking and without anything getting squashed. Somehow, I had managed to live to my ripe old age without squashing yoghurts.

Another trolley arrived, "That's for Sue and the lodge. Just got Morag's to get now. Don't mix them up." What was I saying about getting to a ripe old age. Does experience count for nothing?

"Last one. Oh that does look very neat and ordered. Well done. I never thought to ask but did you want anything?"

"I need some shaving gear and some wine." extracting my shopping bag from the pocket of the back door.

"I need to fill up and then call at the chandlers for a couple of pieces then I will take you shopping."

Taking the alternative route around the Firth we arrived at Beauly on the river of the same name. I knew a lovely delicatessen cafe on the main square aptly named Corner on the Square for a delightful lunch and shopping for deli items.

The Square Beauly

Across the road was Campbells of Beauly, Country tailor and outfitters. According to their website "Campbell's retail emporium is an experience in itself with a truly original and characterful charm to its rustic and vintage appearance. The alchemy of the original fixtures and fittings from 1858 with the contemporary products sold today makes for both a unique appearance and experience."

It is certainly a cut above the rest, with a rare selection of quality, out of the ordinary clothes. Fair Isle gloves and beret, fingerless mittens, jumpers and, lots of tweed, in fact everything you would not need for a Caribbean cruise.

Campbell's of Beauly

Penny was in her element purring like a contented cat in a warm snugly bed. "These gloves would be ideal to keep your fingers warm when chopping logs dear." I suggested loudly for the benefit of the rather prim and proper sales assistants, receiving a kick on my shins for my cheek.

After much umming and aahing she set her sights on the Fair Isle gloves and beret and could not be persuaded to buy a Donegal yarn cable crew neck jumper. As she pulled it over her head her strawberry locks fell onto her shoulders, folding her arms snuggling into it. The label said 'a casual look on a freezing cold Winter's day.'

I cannot justify that on a single jumper." she whispered.

Picking up the gloves and beret I raced her to the till whipping my credit card out first, despite her protestations. "Go and have a look in the artist's gallery next door while I get these wrapped."

"Ready for home?"

She nodded as we set off back along the most scenic snaking

route to our version of civilisation. First stop was Morag's, who was most grateful for her boxes of shopping and the mackerel.

Next was the Croft where I left Penny unpacking while I delivered to Sue. When I returned the kettle was on ready for tea and shortbread.

"Are you off to the boat with your bits and pieces?"

"No. They can wait till the morning. I found this in the car by the way." handing her the Campbell's bag.

For once, she was almost speechless but came round to tell me off and thank me for my gift. Finally, she held it across her body embracing it as she looked in the mirror and then a warm appreciative hug.

Next morning we lay in bed with our mugs of tea watching the sunrise through the window. "I think I might call in sick today Penny. I don't feel like going to work."

"I have already told them I will be off all week with Covid." she laughed.

The joy of retirement is to do what you want, when you want, provided the phone doesn't ring or there is a knock at the door by a friend in need. However, in my short time there I had realised how much we needed each other in our miniscule community, so helping was not considered work.

Doris was now in use regularly throughout the week, fishing, lobster pots and even a late night voyage to lie back in the boat viewing the Northern Lights flickering and dancing across the sky in vast sheets and curtains of blues and greens. The lobster pots proved quite prolific, only one or two at a time, but more than we needed so I decided to make a holding cage on the end of the pontoon. At the lodge scrap bin, I found large galvanised bakery trays that I lashed together with numerous cable ties, suspending it on rope from the pontoon. Lobster and crab were quite happy in our living larder fed on fish carcasses. Razor clams kept well in a smaller container inside along with scallops also surviving a temporary reprieve from the sauté pan. In fact, it was far superior to the freezer. I did try live Pollock and a sea trout but they seemed to thrash about so much and were a handful to retrieve so I reverted to the traditional priest.

Scallop

Joe was always keen to accept a fishing invitation and I met Murdo, Morag's son, for the first time on leave from agricultural college. Joe was a mine of stories of the old days whereas Murdo had a modern perspective on life out there in the real world where he had to earn a living. He knew the best fishing spots for sea trout and salmon and the brown trout in the lochs above so I was keen to tap his knowledge.

LANDY AND THE MERMAID'S POOL

I think Millie the Mini and Anja were a little jealous of Doris getting all the attention and action. They barely turned a wheel. I thought we could take Doris further afield on the trailer and made enquiries about a tow bar for Anja. Then I thought about the Landrover, surely it must have one.

I hadn't noticed previously in my rush to uncover Doris, but the Landy seemed unusually high. Penny and I stripped the tarpaulin back to find it was on axle stands, wheels off the ground and had been prepared for storage. There was even a mechanics sliding bed on wheels so I could inspect the chassis, infamous for its ability to rust, but this one was; waxed, greased and oiled to the hilt.

Lightweight Landrover

"You had better ask Alex and Joe to give you a hand getting it back on the ground." Penny advised. She was right. I managed to turn the wheels so the brakes had not seized on and the handbrake and footbrake worked but there was no battery to test the electrics. The radiator had been drained but there was oil in the sump.

Alex brought a spare battery and a charger eager to play with any Landrover. For a dour moorland keeper he was most animated and vociferous, telling me it was air portable, a lightweight military version lifted by helicopter on a pallet. "It's mint. Look at the mileage under 5000. It's never been anywhere or done any hard work. It's worth a fortune."

I had considered its value on the market as a classic barn find but Penny and I decided we did not need the money and it could be put to better use here.

With the aid of a trolley jack, we managed to lower it off the axle stands front, then rear and roll it in to the daylight. Unusually it was a 24v system; Alex pointing out it had been a radio command vehicle, where the rear was fitted with a full width radio cage, small table and a seat for the operator. With battery installed, the ignition lights illuminated and the electrics appeared in order.

Alex turned it over by hand to ensure it was not seized and coat the dry bearings with oil. With spark plugs removed, it was easy to turn the engine with the starting handle. We left one plug out to check for a spark and Alex held it close to the engine block while I turned the ignition key and pressed the starter. Success, we had a bright blue spark. Dinking the petrol tank with a spanner indicated it was near full but Alex undid the drain plug to test for rust. All was well apart from the foul smell of stale petrol.

The first few turns had no effect but we assumed it was drawing petrol through the fuel line and carburettor. Alex went to his Landrover returning with an aerosol of highly volatile starting spray for reluctant engines. The air filter on the carburettor, full of cobwebs, was soon cleaned. A good jet down the air inlet and the Landy burst into life with a grumble and clouds of blue smoke. After a lot of backslapping, we stopped for coffee letting her idle and warm up.

All seemed in good order so it was time for a test run up the glen road and back. Alex advised that I check for oil and petrol leaks from dried out gaskets, and watch for perished water hoses. He had contacts for the spares and took notes of the chassis and engine numbers. Other than an oil change and antifreeze, the Landy seemed good to go. If she broke down around here, it was a short journey home.

Further exploration of the workshop uncovered a black and white photograph of the beach. Closer examination in the daylight revealed a large speck on the the ridge of the promontory close to the observation post. It was Landy.

Over a week later, Alex delivered the spares leaving me to change all the hoses and top up the antifreeze. I started the engine every day and managed a trip up and down the glen road testing for leaks but all was well.

Even Penny managed a modicum of interest and excitement at the possible uses beyond towing Doris; collecting logs from the brae, 4x4 when snowbound, off-road to the observation point and all the other moorland tracks, opening up endless painting opportunities, fishing in the lochs, helping Alex on the moor, rabbiting and possibly helping with the grouse and stalking.

"So we have my Anja and your Millie the Mini. What is the Landy to be called?"

"Male or female?

"Well Landy is a roughty-toughty military utility workhorse so probably male."

"Landy. Just Landy. That's what father called him."

So Landy it was.

We did need to get rid of the stale fuel so I proposed a trip to see Rob and Mary in Laide to use it up, calling at Ullapool for fresh petrol on the way back. I suggested we could take her crafts to the community cafe and have lunch. Jessie could come to. Millie the Mini was automatic so Penny would benefit from driving a manual, especially a less powerful vehicle working up and down the box on the Highland hills.

"It's only forty miles." I persuaded, knowing it would seem like eighty, but she accepted the challenge.

The following Saturday, I had Landy warming up outside loaded with spares, a jerry can, water, tools and a bed for Jessie. Penny made a flask and packed some cake for the journey just in case. I had considered taking some Pollock and shellfish but they were too valuable to us as food.

After a few gear crunching miles Penny got the hang of the gear change, but found the steering a little vague and the brakes nowhere near as effective as the Mini. She soon learnt to anticipate hazards and bends so she could slow down in time. It was a scenic run along Loch Broom and Little Loch Broom and then the coast at Gruinard Bay. Stopping several times for pictures, a run for Jessie and a cup of tea, our one hour trip was nearer two arriving at 11am. Thankfully, the petrol gauge seemed to be working and we had enough for the return to Ullapool.

Rob had been on lookout and rushed to greet me with a warm handshake, whilst looking at Penny. Mary joined us and I got a hug before introductions began in earnest. Penny and Mary took the arts and crafts into the hall and I brought Jessie on the lead. Rob was most keen to learn more about Penny and the life I was creating with her in our small community. Not only could he not believe how lucky I had been to find such an attractive soul mate but he was astounded at my Burns Night activities.

"Rob, they asked me because all the men were at the Highland show and, taking your advice I didn't say 'No'"

The hall was buzzing with locals and a few tourists checking out the stalls. Homemade bread and cakes, shortbread, venison sausage rolls, smoked salmon, honey, preserves, knitted crafts and clothes. Penny set out her craft offerings, mead and jars of honey on a table and was soon surrounded by admiring customers. One interested party was the polis, Constable McKinnon, who I had seen at the Ceilidh on my first visit.

"You have some nice wee crafts here."

"We like to support the community if we can. I came to the Ceilidh not long ago with Rob and Mary."

"Och aye." He replied picking up a bottle of mead. "Is this alcoholic by any chance?"

"Yes." responded Penny. "I make it myself from my own honey; it's fermented like homemade wine."

There was a long "Ayeeeee" In response. "You need a licence to sell it, but not to give it away." advised the polis. "I've never tried mead myself but I think Mrs McKinnon would like it as she has a sweet tooth."

I could see where this was going, "Well by all means have a sample for Mrs McKinnon with our compliments." stopping Penny from intervening with a kick on the ankle.

"Och that's most kind of you. Thank you very much. I'm sure she will be delighted. Well that's me done for the day now; I'll leave you to get on with your **sales**, aye." The Polis emphasising '**sales.**'

Penny was about to spit feathers at me as I raised my hand, "Oiling the wheels darling. Oiling the wheels. One never knows when we might need his help or a blind eye."

Rob and I wandered outside to marvel at Landy and to hear about Doris and my fishing exploits. "You have certainly dropped on your feet. Sounds like paradise to me."

Lunch was soup and hot sausage or bacon rolls followed by fruit pie. We sat and ate together, with frequent, yet pleasant interruptions from the friendly locals.

"Anyone know who that Landrover outside belongs to? Came a shout from the door. I was fear-struck that someone had crashed into it, or rolled away or was on fire.

"That's Gordon from the garage." Rob advised.

Gordon was easily identified by his oily overalls and a well-worn tweed cap made shiny with years of grease and representing a significant fire hazard. He was yet another Landrover enthusiast. They are insulted if one refers to them as fanatics. Gordon wanted to know everything about Landy, amazed at its condition and low mileage and the military number plates. He appeared to be working up to a value but I made it clear it was not mine to sell and part of the family. He understood and offered his services anytime, as he was an expert on Landrovers.

The sale ended about 3pm and we helped clear the hall, stacking tables and chairs. It had been lovely to meet Rob and Mary and Penny invited them up for the day, so the boys could fish and the girls could talk girl talk.

Penny offered to drive back, refuelling in Ullapool for the last leg home. Landy seemed to perform a little better with fresh petrol coursing through her pipes and finally burning off all the residual oil in the engine.

"How was that drive for you?

"My arms are weary with the lack of power steering. We take such things for granted in modern cars don't we? Everything is so basic but practical and good fun."

"Now that you've mastered on-road, what about driving off-road? We have only been in two-wheel drive so far."

"Yes I'm up for that."

"How about fishing the lochan and you drive up the brae?"
"You mean the Mermaid's Pool." She replied with an air of mystery.
"Tell me more."
"There are several legends about the pool, thought to be used in ancient Celtic water worship rituals. People say the waters offer healing qualities to those brave enough to bathe in them. For those looking for eternal life, the best time to visit is at midnight at Easter, the only time of the year when the Mermaid is said to appear. If she looks upon you fondly then she will grant you the gift of immortality. Make sure you catch her on a good day though, otherwise you may be pulled into the pool to your death!"
"Sounds like a good yarn for the visitors to the lodge, especially the Americans. Let's hope we live till Easter then."

With Landy loaded with tackle and Jessie, we set off for the lochan one late balmy afternoon. Landy has several levers with coloured knobs so Penny selected the red one to engage low-box, automatically engaging four-wheel drive and set off at a slow grinding crawl up the brae.

The tracks created by Angus and Davy collecting timber for Penny terminated at the end of the trees lining the burn, so we were now in open country, boggy holes, ditches, heather-hidden boulders, but there was the semblance of a footpath or sheep track. Occasionally I jumped out to check the ground but we edged ever nearer our destination.

Brown trout were leaping for large dry flies, probably sedges, as Penny took her father's old fly rod and stood at the water's edge in deep contemplation.
"Can I put my arm around you and hold your hand?"
"I thought we had come to fish." She retorted.
"I was just going to help you cast."
"Ok then."
Standing behind her, I placed my right hand over hers on the rod handle and the other hand and line in my left. It was a most pleasant position to be in, smelling her perfumed hair and pressing gently against her cheek.

"Lift the rod gently then power it up sharply to twelve o clock and stop. Don't panic about the line behind you but count to three. You will feel it tug the rod then drive the rod forward and stop at ten o'clock and your line should sing out." I instructed.

"Sounds easy enough. Let me have a go."

Penny made a beautiful cast, laughing "See I told you it was easy."

She did it again.

"You know how to cast don't you?" I exclaimed.

"Father taught me years ago."

"I should have asked shouldn't I? Lesson learned. I'll leave you to it then."

"First one to catch is the winner!" she taunted.

I watched as she changed the dry, deer hair sedge I had tied on for her, and then cast to circles on the flat calm water where fish were sipping flies from the surface tension. A gentle take as the fish turned to head down, her line tightened, the rod bowed as she played the first fish, drawing it to the net, rod held high, net in her left hand and gracefully scooping the fish.

My line was not even wet and I was too embarrassed to ask her what fly she was using so I tried a small black spider.

As I walked along the bank, I heard a shriek and looking back saw her rod bent over.

"Beginner's luck obviously." I chuntered enviously to myself.

I managed to get my line out before she caught another, but I was now in the wrong frame of mind, as my casting thrashed the water, instead of caressing the surface, scaring any sensible trout away.

Mermaid's Pool

I walked to the waterfall, a grey mare's tail, tumbling about fifty feet into the edge of the lochan where, over the years, it had gouged a deep pool, a dark black, inky black, mirror gently rippling and reflecting the rays of the setting red sun.

Something was moving out there. I could see a line, a wake in the water as a fish moved underneath. I watched for some time trying to gauge its next move. What would tempt this fish, possibly a large specimen? A Daddy long-legs, a large hook with long body tied to it. Legs were filaments from a cock pheasant's tail knotted to look like leg joints and two hackle tips for wings. Sometimes something big and out of the ordinary does the trick.

Crane Fly

I gauged the distance not wanting to creep up on the fish in a series of splashy casts. I made false casts in the air until I had the distance and dropped the big daddy gently on the water. I saw the wake turn sharply and accelerate to the fly and an explosion as a white mouth opened to devour it and dive solidly hooking itself in the scissor of its jaw. With my rod bent and held high, my taut line was zipping away into the depths of the pool. I had to play this one gently on such light tackle as this fish could easily snap the cast.

We tugged and pulled at each other for a long time as I prayed my knot would hold, and then the mighty brown trout rocketed from the depths, breaking surface, leaping and shaking its head before crashing into the water. My line fell loose. The mighty fish, a leviathan, had won, and taken my daddy with him.

"That was a shame. He was a good fish." Penny sympathised. Better than my four small ones."

"A bird in the hand Penny. I thought it was the mermaid trying to pull me in! He will be there for another day. He is a challenge."

"I'm going for a swim. Coming?"

"I might as well join him if I can't catch him or even a little one. Just put my gear away."

Penny walked round to the back of the waterfall stripping behind a falling shower curtain then walking forward under the cascade, holding her arms aloft forming a perfect Y. I watched in awe for many seconds at her beauty, her shapeliness, as she looked up into the tumbling water before diving into the inky blackness and rippling the setting sun. What a picture that would make?

I followed suit but with a far less dramatic or artistic entry. I just bombed in off the edge and showered briefly in the mare's tail. What an experience to equal, nay surpass that of Ben Fogle. After a few circuits of the pool Penny was back behind the waterfall towelling herself dry.
"Come on we have trout to cook for supper!"

I had to ask her about her deadly fly and, taking a small battered tin fly box bearing her father's name from her pocket, she revealed his collection of favourite flies."
"Was it a little black gnat?"
"His favourite. And he tied them as well."
"Did I see you singing in the shower?"
"No not singing. I was telling father I had caught fish with his fly. I also told him I was with a kind, gentle, caring, man that I love."
This time it was my turn to wipe the moisture from my eyes.
"He loves you very much as well."

CHARLIE PARKES

Penny in the Mermaid's Pool

PANDORA'S BOX?

Following the removal of Doris and Landy from the barn, we had several exploratory rummages as to what other secrets could be unearthed. It was secure with no windows or roof lights and hefty padlocks held the heavy doors well and truly shut.

Across the end was a full length wooden workbench, and mounted on the wall above, metal cubby hole racks painted with Army issue olive drab, sequentially numbered containing a miscellany of useful bits and bobs. Two angle poise lamps improved lighting over the bench.

Underneath were numerous wooden crates with military markings that would need further examination when I had nothing to do, perhaps in the short days of winter. Two paraffin heaters would take the chill off. I instantly recognised one open-sided crate from my early police days, dragging it into the daylight. Noticing the light was on in the bathroom, mischief was afoot, as I cranked the handle building the siren up to a crescendo wailing an air raid warning. Penny charged round the corner scared out of her wits. She had been sitting on the toilet but at least she had a good sense of humour, retreating with a wagging finger and "Yoooooooooooou!"

Hand Cranked Air Raid Siren and WB400 Receiver

I explained over tea that I had to test air raid sirens and the grey plastic box on her windowsill next to the telephone, as part of civil defence measures.

"The Speaking Clock?" Penny questioned.

It resembled an old style telephone base but had no handset, just a speaker grille and a volume knob. The WB400 was the means by which speech and warning signals could be sent to the various warning points.

"My annual task was to notify all the locations on our patch of a forthcoming test when a message would be broadcast for them to record, demonstrating that the telephone network was in working order. The system was a civil defence communications network designed to keep on working even if parts were blown up. In peacetime, you get the speaking clock."

"Now we have the siren we could give the neighbours a four minute warning if Putin presses the button."

"What could we do in four minutes?" enquired Penny, a cheeky and mischievous look on her face.

Several Jerry cans were labelled petrol, paraffin and two-stroke. Numerous drums contained a variety of oils and greases.

A large metal, olive drab cabinet with drawers below housed a most useful and substantial tool set. Welding bottles mounted on a trolley, a variety of hydraulic jacks, farm jacks and ramps added to the complete workshop, enough tools and equipment for me to start a repair shop, if I had the skills and the inclination.

In the far corner, a heavy-duty metal cabinet caught my eye. Thick metal walls and doors secured top and bottom with mortise locks and the whole thing bolted to the wall. There was no way I could lever the doors open so I had to find the keys. Before starting a lengthy search, I asked Penny if she had any more keys and was directed to the drawer in the kitchen cabinet. I believed I was looking for a pair of similar five lever keys and searched through the flotsam and jetsam deposited there over the years. Finally, pushing to the back, I found such a pair tied with string to a worn and torn luggage label bearing a faint scribbled "Guns N Ammo" Bingo!

Would this be a treasure chest or Pandora's box? Only one way to find out I thought as the keys unlocked top and bottom. Several brown metal ammunition boxes sat on shelves down the right hand side neatly labelled .762 and .22.

This was obviously the armoury. On the left were two racks, one above the other containing several items wrapped in waxed or oiled paper. The shapes indicated standard army issue SLRs firing the .762 NATO round. Serious stuff.

There were also two 303 bolt action rifles but the barrels had been converted, tubed with a smaller .22 barrel for training. One with open sights, and the other with a telescopic sight. One further rifle, that I did not recognise, was fitted with a superior looking scope and I suspected it was a sniper's rifle.

Phew. What should we do with this lot? Start a war? Assassinate Putin? Lock the cabinet and plead ignorance? I locked up. They would be useful in the event of civil unrest to protect and survive or plink a few rabbits for dinner. Careful thought was required.

Telling Penny of my find she seemed quite unsurprised asking, "Did you find any hand grenades?"

"Hand grenades?"

"Yes father found a case of them in there years ago?"

"What did he do with those?"

"Oh we buried them just over the wall in the brae and planted a tree on them."

"I had better check, but I guess father will have found them all."

Penny agreed. "Were there any rockets?"

"Rockets? Do you mean missiles?"

"Oh no! I always thought they were fireworks, no pretty lights, just a flash and the most enormous bang."

"Maroons. You must mean maroons. Signal rockets."

"Father always let one off at 11am on Remembrance Day for the two minute silence to begin."

Possessing unauthorised firearms, especially prohibited army issue weapons, can attract a lot of unwanted attention and difficult questions. Why did her father keep the firearms? If this was to be his bunker then I can understand him using them to defend against foreign invaders, or even looters, if the country was in total lawless chaos, but why bury the grenades. I also understood him keeping the sniper rifle for deer and the .22 converted .303 for rabbits but the SLRs have only one purpose – to shoot humans! Or, perhaps with the Cold War threat diminishing and the prospect of world peace dawning, he decided to lock the guns away and forget them.

Should I let sleeping dogs lie? Should I tell the police or the army? My thoughts ran to the PC McKinnon, the polis who enjoyed late drinking in the hotel at Laide and our mead. Could he help? Or, do like father did, dig a hole and plant another tree. Further checks failed to uncover, grenades, rockets or anything explosive, just the live ammunition.

We could ask Angus to dig us a hole with his JCB but we felt the exercise would do us both good. In some whisky-fed moment there was bound to be a blabbermouth leaking the information to the "jungle bagpipes." Maybe it would be best to leave them securely locked in the cabinet, "just in case" so that is where they stayed and I hid the keys by screwing them on top of a rafter. It would be easy to plead ignorance in the future and blame father.

GLORIOUS TWELFTH

Red grouse - Lagopus lagopus scotica

After a long hot and sunny summer, the Summer Isles were easing into autumn. Our skinny-dipping sessions grew less and less as a chill wind blew in and the sun hid behind the clouds. We were both keen to dive for scallops and now we had Doris we could find and locate the scallop beds, but even at low tide they remained several metres down. Wet suits, snorkels, and a glass-bottomed bucket were the answer.

I have never had such a slim profile in many years, held tightly in place by a giant rubber tube. To be fair I had lost weight, toned up and alleviated my back problem through diet and exercise. Being partly self-sufficient requires a lot of effort, chopping logs, hauling the boat and lobster pots, walking to my sea trout spot and so on. Penny was the obvious choice to dive. She was an accomplished swimmer and submerged easily with a couple of house bricks tied round her waist! I kept her on a light line in case of accidents but all went well and she was able to dislodge a handful for a meal. No more than we needed. We marked the beds with her orange buoys tied to a brick. We were not concerned that anyone would raid our beds as the kayakers paddling round the islands explored the many caves and inlets, but seldom invaded the beach and the bay. It was our beach. Getting back on board was difficult so I would throw her the line and tow her in as she performed her water ballet or synchronised swimming.

Landy was busy gathering timber from the brae to be logged and dried for the following winter. It was also the start of the grouse season and Alex had been very busy putting the finishing touches to the grouse butts and counting birds. The Lodge was ready for shooting parties and the return of the owner's family for their day on the moor.

Alex and I were now quite friendly through his help with Landy, and his father Joe was a constant fishing companion. I was hoping for a chance to act as loader on shoot days, standing with one of the guns, but I knew that was a privileged position due to the cash rewards and hierarchy among the shoot's casual employees. Neighbouring keepers worked together loading on each other's moors, so opportunities were likely to be rare. Beating was beyond even my rejuvenated physique but I thought I might be able to help with refreshments, morning elevenses, sloe gins and sloegasms, so awaited the invitation.

When it came, it was quite a surprise. Alex called to see me, asking if I would load for Mr St John Sinclair the owner of the lodge and the moor. His wife would also be present in the butt. Mr Sinclair had specifically asked if I would load for him so he could get to know the "Honorary Scot" who was now a regular performer at the Lodge Burns Evenings.

"Alex. I don't want to put anybody's nose of joint...."

"You won't. Big Jock, from the neighbouring moor, fell down a rabbit hole and is out of commission." Alex gave me a thorough briefing and was obviously a little nervous at my involvement.

Penny and I arrived at The Lodge in good time to collect Mr Sinclair's guns and cartridges, plus the baskets of soup and elevenses. Landy was last in a line of smart, highly polished Range Rovers to be led by Mr Sinclair. It was to be playtime off-road and all part of the fun. We were introduced to Mr Sinclair and his wife, Samantha, both delightful people, "Rabbie Burns I assume?" was his opening line with a laugh, "and of course we know Penny."

"Mr Sinclair."

"Please call me St John."[pronounced sin jun]

At the first drive, I laid his guns in the heather on the front wall of the butt, hooking the cartridge bag over my shoulder in readiness. I suggested a quick practice to exchange guns and then loaded ready for the grouse to fly in. Grouse drives often include a lot of waiting as the beaters cover long distances over difficult terrain to drive the birds.

"Are you by any chance related to Archibald Sinclair?"

"Oh the liberal politician? Viscount of Thurso?"

"That's the one."

"No I'm afraid not, although I do get asked from time to time. Why do you ask?"

"I write books and in my research came across the Viscount, where it was said he could not find boots nor shoes that did not hurt his feet, so tramped barefoot on the moor at some considerable pace."

"That takes a lot of guts."

"It does and there were no Landrovers or quad bikes in those days."

"What were you researching?"

"It was an item on the railways opening up Scotland in the 1800s and building isolated halts, miles from anywhere in what was called terra incognita, uncharted land. I came across William Adams book Twenty Six Years Reminiscences of Scottish Grouse Moors. He had to build a four mile road to connect a halt to his lodge."

Glancing to my left I saw the flankers flag waving turning the grouse towards us, flying fast, flying low, four in a diamond pattern hugging the contours, heading across us and to our right

"Forward!"

St John had them. Gun in shoulder, leaning forward, he fired twice and two birds dropped thirty yards in front. Then springing upright, he exchanged guns whipping round to the rear following the second brace as they flew between butts. Remounting his gun he fired two shots as they went away, falling into the heather in puffs of feathers.

"Good shooting St John." A loader likes to see the gun shoot well especially if he has been able to point out a bird the gun has not seen, and conducted a rapid and safe exchange. It all helps when the time comes for the golden handshake.

"A brace in front and behind. Good job you saw them coming."

We soon gelled in the butt working well handling double guns, exchanging an empty gun for a loaded one, with an almost rhythmic synchronised timing, without clanking the barrels on a pair of very expensive shotguns. We enjoyed each other's company and he knew many of the people I knew through shooting. I gleaned he was public school, Cambridge, then working for his father's stockbroker firm in the City, married well and inherited well with Eden House, a farming estate in Wiltshire and Gàradh Eden Lodge with 20,000 acres.

It was time for elevenses after two drives and as Field Butler, I assisted Penny, to distribute drinks, venison sausage rolls, mini pasties and Bullshot, a hot beef consommé, a clear soup, served with a splash of vodka or pale, dry sherry.

One more drive and then the guns retired for lunch to a dark and drafty stone building high on the hill with trestle tables and benches. Sue and Penny served a superb buffet, mainly cold cuts and pies with, salads, smoked salmon and hot boiled potatoes with fruit pie and cream to follow. I sat outside with Alex who was keen to know if the master was pleased.

After lunch, Mr Sinclair came to look at Landy. He was an aficionado, having had many such vehicles in his lifetime but not one quite like Landy. He scrutinised every inch and even lay on the heather to look underneath. "Charles. Could I ask a favour?"

"Certainly."

"Would you let me drive Landy?"

"But of course. What about your Range Rover?"

"Samantha can manage that. Perhaps Penny could travel with her."

Mr Sinclair led the line of Range Rovers to the final drive in our old Landy, somewhat less comfortable but infinitely more enjoyable.

There were drinks after the last drive, counting the bag and most importantly expressing thanks and appreciation to the beaters and pickers up. Mr Sinclair again led the crocodile back to the Lodge for tea but took a detour,

"Watch this Charles. This will be a tester for them." He chortled, heading for a narrow gap in a stone wall. Landy was significantly narrower than a standard Landover and even more so than its big brother Range Rover. His speed of approach worried me slightly as we neared the gap. Those behind us were unable to see the opening clearly. Mr Sinclair charged through then swung round to watch the fun. Wing mirrors were turned in, some drivers got out to weigh up the width, others had all their cameras switched on and cagily edged their way through, some with wives and girlfriends in front waving them on. Mr Sinclair thought it most entertaining although he did catch a disapproving stare from Samantha.

Landy had proved most useful carrying Mr and Mrs Sinclair, their guns and paraphernalia. We cleaned the guns in the gunroom, always something of a frenzy as each loader is trying to finish quickly, ensuring they do not miss the golden handshake, "a tip" for their labours. Mr Sinclair called the guns away from their drinks and the log fire, filing them in to shake and deliver. My handshake was a particularly warm and rewarding one with the added bonus of appreciation for my role on Burn's Night. I think I had made a friend.

"Do you ever get down to Wiltshire Charles?"

"I have been that way but mostly Yorkshire down to Belvoir and

Chatsworth."

Alex comes down to my estate for a couple of day's shooting towards the end of the season. You must come with him. You may get a chance at an English Gentleman. Bring Penny as well. I am sure Samantha will love to take her shopping."

ROB AND THE LEVIATHAN

With all my other activities, I had neglected my salmon and sea trout fishing. Penny was keen to continue her secret painting and replace the craft items she had sold at the lodge, and Laide community sale. She also needed more scallop shells so Penny donning her wet suit, gathered enough for a dinner with Rob and Mary who were due to stay with us. They arrived mid morning and I guess Rob was keen to get fishing and I was ready to oblige.

Doris bobbed gently over the kelp bed as we had a great session catching Pollock and some newly arrived Cod. We spent the afternoon filleting our catch and resting ready for an evening session on the river pool.

Penny insisted on a hot meal before we left knowing we would be out late and had arranged an evening soirée for Sue, Isla and Morag to enjoy a good gossip.

Rob had eyed the channel enviously during our session in Doris but the tide was now an hour off full flood. I gave him first cast and he started his sweep down the channel as the sun sank below the promontory, the moon hiding behind a cloud. I sat and watched his expert casting, his line flowing out softly and quietly across the pool. Suddenly there was an explosion as a large fish leapt from the water with Rob's fly hooked in its jaw. Rob lifted his rod trying to maintain contact with the fish by tightening the line. The fish dived then ran away at speed with Rob letting out line steadily until the fish slowed, then sank to the bottom tugging and shaking its head to rid itself of the hook. "Salmon I think Charles."

Rob maintained a tight line waiting for the immovable object to succumb to the irresistible force. The line slackened as the fish ran at Rob who, by now had edged to the bank winding the slack line in to regain contact. The fish turned and ran again. Gradually Rob wore the fish down sliding him towards the shore where I waited to slip the net under him.

It was a salmon, fresh run as indicated by the presence of sea lice. It was also a wild one and not an escapee from the salmon farm near the island in the bay. It was a male, a cock fish, if it had been a female we would have released her to ascend the river to spawn on the redds, completing the lifecycle. Rob was delighted with his first salmon of the season meriting a swig of malt from his hip flask.

It was my time to wet a line and I was going to try a new method with a spinning rod and a small spoon with a sliver of silver mackerel skin on a treble hook. As a boy on one of our caravan holidays to Aberdeen, I fished the River Don where it crossed the beach in a sandy channel. Using the same tackle, I had seen an angler take two sea trout but it proved irresistible to a variety of flatfish. Casting out I let it hit the far side of the channel and then wound in slowly trying to attract a flattie from the sandy bed, or a wary sea trout.

Several casts later, my rod bent double with a violent wobbling. Rob made ready with the net and the first of several plaice dropped in my wicker creel. We thought it might be diplomatic to return and spend some time with the ladies and discuss our achievements over several tots of malt.

Wild salmon command a premium if one wants to sell and find a market. Rob advised getting it smoked commercially, but warned that I might not get back the fish I took in! Or, I could make a cold smoker. That sounded fun and Rob invited me to look at his homemade version. We agreed he would take the fish, smoke it and we would share the results. Penny and I love smoked salmon with scrambled egg.

"Did you enjoy your girly night?"

"It was great to have some female company and talk girl talk." she said.

"You didn't miss me and my small talk then?"

"No darling sorry."

Seeing my look of disappointment and rejection, she continued the pain,

"I'm am sorry. I would truly like to make love to you rather than talk, but the walls are a bit thin and the bed is very creaky and springy as you know. We can't keep our guests awake can we?"

"Or give them something to gossip about. Anyway Rob and I are going to make a fish smoker….."

"Oh! bor…….ing. I am feeling so sleepy." She yawned, turning away from me, and rolling on her side, took my right arm folding it round her in a hug.

"Love you though. Lots. Night darling."

The next day Rob and I walked the brae to fish the Mermaid's Pool. He was keen to know more about my relationship with Penny especially how it established so quickly.

"We both took your advice never to say no."

"My advice?

"Yes. We met while I was fishing, I caught a good Pollock and offered her half. She said 'yes.' I plucked up courage asking her to join me for dinner round my campfire. She said 'yes'. She asked me to the croft for dinner the next evening. I said 'yes.' We had dinner and a pleasant evening, a bottle of Margaux and some damson gin. She took me by the hand and said 'You can't say no.'
"So what did you say?"
"Nothing, Rob. I said nothing. The next morning she suggested I move in. I said 'yes' so you see it's all your fault."

"Well I never! You jammy bas……."
"I know. I know. I keep pinching myself to see if I am dreaming."
"I can see I need to try taking my own advice."
"Let's try and catch Leviathan."

It was a cool and breezy overcast day and the pool seemed blacker than ever in the shadow of the cliff behind the mare's tail. Nothing seemed to be moving and no sign of any flies hatching, so we crept to the edge of Leviathan's Lair to see if he was in. I had been back several times on my own to catch him only to see his gaping white mouth laughing at me as he leapt from the water my Daddy long legs still stuck in his jaw.

"Rob" I whispered," when I was a lad we were on holiday in Scotland on a caravan site and in the local paper was a story of a monster trout in a wee burn next to the site. Everyone had tried everything to catch him without success, until an eight old lad deceived him with a cold chip."

"Never? Really? A chip?"

"I had Leviathan first time with a Daddy but I bet he won't take another."

"I bet he's a cannibal, could be a Ferox. Big trout live off other fish, tadpoles, frogs and anything that falls in the water they can get in their jaws. They even eat mice."

Rob ferreted in his kit bag bringing out the biggest most colourful box of huge gaudy reservoir flies. For trout fishing, I would normally have a small Orvis plastic box that floated and fitted snugly in a vest pocket. This box was A4 size.

Mouse Fly

"Let's try a mouse fly Charles. They reckon this will wake that monster up. Plop it through the surface film and strip the line in fast and wait for the action to begin." He enthused.

"Have you ever used one Rob?"

"Not at £5 a fly. Too darn expensive if you lose it." He laughed.

"Rob. You may have the honour of extracting Leviathan from the deep."

Rob was delighted to take the opportunity and I made ready with my mobile phone to capture the event for posterity.

There was no sign of his tell-tale wake so we assumed he was several feet down waiting for an unsuspecting animal to be his next meal.

Rob cast the mouse across the pool, landing with quite a plop, unlike the delicate landing of a tiny dry fly. The plop would attract attention and roust Leviathan into action. On our knees, we waited with baited breath and anticipation as Rob stripped his line back in at speed towing the waterskiing mouse and creating a wake. If this were a Batman movie, there would be a great "Kerpow" as action went into slow-motion. Leviathan emerged at forty five degrees through the surface film, huge white mouth agape, his long broad back a deep shade of greeny-black, his sides of tawny yellow speckled with black spots surrounded by red halos, leaping high in the air, shaking his head before re entering the pool on his side sending waves across the water. Rob let the line flow steadily though his hand as we waited to see if Leviathan was free or not. The line was tight, Rob holding it steady but gently, feeling for any movement.

Once again, Leviathan surfaced standing on his tail and walking across the surface tugging for his freedom before diving once again. Leviathan tried several more times leaping, tail-walking, flopping and twisting but the hook was well fixed and the knot remained sound. Finally, Leviathan floated to the surface, spent, lying on his side to be towed, rather ignominiously for such a fish, to the net, like an obsolete destroyer being towed to the salvage yard.

We whooped, hollered and patted each other on the back very briefly as he lay in the net. Rob thought he was a large brown trout gone cannibal, as the pond was probably not big enough to sustain a Ferox. Coup de grace or let him go? We decided to put him back, deserving of his freedom and we could try for him another day. We guessed his weight at over ten pounds and probably of considerable age. I retrieved the remains of my Daddy-longlegs fly from his jaw as Rob collected him from the net holding him upright in the water, watching his jaws gasping and pushing cold fresh oxygenated water through his gills. Slowly his body twitched and he was ready to go. Flicking his powerful fan-shaped tail the beast of the lochan was free. "And away." We cried in respect.

Anything thereafter would be an anti-climax so it was a slow amble back to the croft to show the girls our video.

DEAR ROLAND!

Autumn had started well but our relationship was to be tested for the first time since my arrival. Seldom did anyone knock on the front door. Locals would open and shout if we were in. Doors were never locked. Dougal the Postie would open the door and throw his post on the kitchen table, have a cup of tea and breakfast if there was any going, but this day he found us round the back and delivered a registered envelope that Penny signed for.

"It's from London. My solicitors I think." She pondered, dropping it on the garden table.

Joe came down for the morning tide so we were off after Pollock. Penny kissed my cheek with "Tight lines."

We were gone a couple of hours returning triumphantly with a good catch. Penny was not about so Landy ran Joe home and I returned to find her, head in hands on the sofa. She had been crying.

"Is it the letter?"

"Yes its bloody Roland. Dear, dear, Roland. The bastard."

She had never mentioned Roland before and I had never heard her swear or get so upset. I awaited further information, if she was willing to divulge it.

"Cup of tea any good?"

She nodded.

The envelope was on the kitchen table and sure enough, it was from Frobisher and Newton, Solicitors London. Penny had the contents on her lap.

Sitting beside her, I gave her a hug and we sipped our tea. "Can I help?"

I turned the tap on and she poured forth a lot of history about Roland, her older brother. She needed to vent her spleen and did so with tearful venom. After the initial volley of insults and examples of what he had done, she apologised and calmed down.

"How about starting with the letter that has upset you so?"

Penny took a deep breath.

"You know I have a flat I rent out in London? I thought the letter was about that, but I also share ownership in my father's flat he used when he worked in London. Roland, my brother, has a half share. He wants to sell it or I give him the money for his share."

"Ok. So it's a question of finding your views then?"

She nodded.

"Roland is an absolute waster. Kicked out of boarding school caught having an affair with the gym mistress, kicked out of university in the second year for failing exams. He's got a masters in women, drink and wasting money on failed business ventures."

There was more to come so I kept my counsel.

"Father financed his ridiculous schemes and then he emigrated to Australia, setting up a business selling and maintaining swimming pools. He wants to be a managing director and let others do the work while he spends the profits, if there are any, and even if there are no profits! This was to be the last scheme father would support. He made that very clear. I think all the worry shortened his life and upset mother dreadfully. When he died father left the flat to Roland and me jointly to share the rent. I put my share into buying my own flat and Roland went down under. I have never heard from the bastard until today. He is back here in England, and wants to see me about the flat, and is trying to contact me through my solicitors, my father's old solicitors."

Penny paused to take stock and get her breath back.

"Can I offer an opinion?"

Penny nodded.

"Putting all the emotion and your dislike for Roland behind you, it seems a simple question of whether you want to sell the flat or not. Do you need the money? You would get a lump sum from the sale, I assume. You are not obliged to see Roland or communicate with him, the solicitors can do all that, and I guess he would take the money and run."

"Yes, you are right but he will just waste it, drink it all away...." Penny was starting to get tearful again.

"When we leave an inheritance to our children we hope they will do something constructive with the riches we bestow on them, but we give them, knowing they can be reckless and foolish with the money we have worked for years to accumulate, being prudent and investing wisely. It is his by right and you cannot control how he spends it."

Penny's head fell on my shoulder resting there quietly for some time.

"I know you are right but ......"

"So what are the options? Simplest option is tell the solicitors to sell, give him his share, charging for the expenses and let him go. Second option is to say no, but then he will bombard you and your solicitors with calls and letters charged to your account at great expense. Remember a lawyer saves your estate from your enemy and keeps it for himself. Lawyers are like woodcocks they both have long bills!"

Penny sat up with a smile. "You are so good at making things simple, being practical. The solicitors have invited me to a meeting with them in London. I think I should go. Will you be Ok here with Jessie?"

"Better ask Jessie?"

"Would you read this letter and perhaps we can draw up a checklist of things to ask?"

The date was set, and I drove Penny to the early morning train in Inverness where we re-enacted Brief Encounter on the platform. It was the first moment of sadness I had experienced since meeting Penny. She arrived safely after an eleven-hour trip, to be met by her friend and old work colleague with whom she would stay, so I was pleased she was not on her own.

The next day was the interview. One feels so helpless without modern communications, a text, a whatsapp, an email even though we managed quite nicely without them at the croft.

On the checklist, I proposed she should insist there be no direct communication between her and Roland and, that he must not be given her contact details. This would also be transmitted to the estate agents. Any communications would be via her solicitors. Penny's evening call was calm and collected resolving to sell up and move on. The solicitor would appoint an estate agent, briefed accordingly, and instruct Roland to find his own solicitor.

Penny was returning the next day and I met her in the late evening running down the platform, not quite in movie-style slow motion, but definitely with emotion. She talked all the way back relieved that the deed was done without any great difficulty or fuss. Or, so we thought.

Paperwork for approval and signing would to be sent to a solicitor in Inverness acting as agent and minimising travel. So Millie and Anja made several journeys dealing with the estate agents, but there was one fly in the ointment as Roland wanted to proceed without a solicitor to cut his costs. Finally, he went to the estate agents and used one of their conveyancers as a cheap option.

Penny was surprised at the starting price of over a million

pounds and even more surprised at the offers. This sweetened the blow of selling the flat but it remained a bitter pill that Roland would waste such a huge sum. They settled on £1,226,000 and Penny was thinking of future spending and investing her share.

"You can buy two jumpers now from Campbells." I jested.

"That gives me an idea." she said slowly and seductively in the mischievous way I had grown accustomed to.

"Going for a shower."

I was reading when I sensed a presence in the doorway. It was Penny, wearing her Fair Isle beret, fingerless gloves and the pullover I bought her from Campbell's. Nothing odd about that you may think but, she wore nothing else!

Next day, a phone call from Frobisher and Newton left Penny annoyed.

"My dear brother has been banging on their door demanding to know where I am. It seems he has put an offer on a bar in Majorca and needs the cash to complete. He wants to sign his half over to me and I pay him out. His conveyancer is ready to go ahead and so are Frobisher but we are waiting to complete a lengthy chain. It could take months even if there are no problems. Frobishers were concerned because he had been drinking and threatened their staff. They had to throw him out."

"It sounds like he doesn't have your details so should be ok for now. But, we ought to have a plan B, an early warning system."

Two days later, there was another devastating call from a very apologetic Mr Frobisher.

"Roland has been to the estate agent on a Saturday morning and conned the young girl on work experience to give him your details. He made some excuse that he was the conveyancer and while working from home had spilt coffee on the papers. He knows my address!"

"He knows your address but not where it is, and it will take him a couple of days to get here. Leave plan B to me and let me answer all telephone calls."

The Croft and the Lodge had been removed from Ordnance Surveys by order of Penny's father and the MOD so finding the cottage would be a challenge requiring local knowledge. I guessed that he would arrive by car or a taxi and would call at the first house to enquire about the Croft. Morag and Angus were the first gatekeepers and our early warning system and alarm. They would delay him by talking Gaelic and then follow him to the Croft. Alex was on standby and loaned the estate radios so we could all communicate.

Hours and days passed then one mid morning Morag radioed that a man in a car was at the farm. They were having communication difficulties as he did not speak Gaelic, but they were sure it was him. He was on his way.

Penny waited in the garden and I secreted myself round the side, out of sight. We heard the car stop, reverse and then turn into the drive.

"So this is where you have been hiding little Sister. Haven't you got a hug for your big brother?" asked Roland in a slightly unfriendly, menacing tone.

Roland was small, heavily built to the extent of being portly and overweight, his garish flowery shirt hanging over his belt. His chubby red complexion indicated Rosacea caused by alcohol, he was unshaven, and his hair curly and unkempt, like his light-coloured, crumpled linen suit.

"Just keep your distance Roland there's no welcome for you here!"

"Don't I get a welcome drink a coffee, or a scotch would be even better."

"Still on the bottle then Roland?"

"Aaww Sis don't be like that. It has been a long time since we have seen each other."

"Let's be clear Roland I don't want to see or hear from you ever.

Why didn't you stay in Australia?"

"Well you know a few financial difficulties; upset some local Aussies and I had to leave a bit quick. And then, there's Luciana my business partner to be. That's why I need the money now Sis, we are buying a bar in Majorca and we need the cash over there by middle of next month."

"Business partner or girlfriend?"

"Well both really. So come on Sis, let's cut a deal and I can be on my way to Majorca never to darken your doorstep again. What are you doing up here alone anyway?"

"That's my business! Bottom line Roland is, I do not have that kind of money and, secondly I'm not going to just hand it over like father did. You can have your share of the flat sale as soon as it completes sooner the better."

"Look you could borrow it, a bridging loan with my half the flat as security. I am prepared to take less than the full amount, a cheque or transfer and some in cash. You would get more than fifty per cent."

"Look Roland I don't need more than my fair share. I don't need my half of the money, but I don't have enough to pay you out and I am not getting a loan. You had better go back to London."

"I have nowhere to live down there Sis. I thought you might put me up for a week or two. Blood's thicker than water Sis."

"Good old Roland every trick in the book until you get what you want. Well it won't work this time. You broke mother's heart when you left and never contacted her again. You shortened father's life with your constant demands for money and you were lucky he left you a share in the flat. By leaving it jointly, he knew there would less chance of you drinking it away. I suppose you have spun Luciana a tale about how rich you are like all the other tarts?"

Roland launched himself towards Penny but stopped dead in his tracks when I stepped out. "Everything all right Penny?"

"Who the …..?"

"This is Charles. He lives here. He's my partner."

"Your partner eh? Never could find anyone to marry you could you? Just a string of live-in lovers." He sneered.

"I think you have said enough Roland."

"Oh you are a posh talking pommie bastard aren't you? This is between me and Penny so keep your toffee nose out of it. Now look Penny, I need that money quick and I am going to keep coming now I know where you are. In fact, I'm going to stay in the car on your doorstep until you agree to sign over. I think I will sit here in your lovely garden and admire your view. I'm sure lover boy here won't do anything about it."

A deep booming voice rang out, "I can do something about it. I think you have outstayed your welcome laddie."

Roland spun round to see Angus; standing arms crossed glaring through his mass of red hair like a Highland bull ready to charge.

"How many more men have you got hidden under your duvet Sis?" he sneered.

"I think there might be two more coming up the drive." She replied spying Alex and Davy.

"Well I ain't shifting and that car's going nowhere!" he screamed throwing the keys over the wall into the brae.

"Nay bother laddie." said Angus, "I will shift it with the fork lift." setting off down the drive as Roland laughed. A laugh that subsided immediately on hearing the roar of the teleporter's diesel engine, seeing a cloud of rising blue smoke and the arms appearing above the wall. The raging bull lowered his horns heading for the car, slipping them under the cills as if it were a pallet. "Are ye leavin or not?"

The arms jumped an inch

"Are ye going?"

The arms jumped another inch

"Wait! Wait! Let me get the keys." cried Roland, leaping over the wall, frantically searching for his keys.

Penny went to the cottage to put the kettle on slightly relieved the ordeal was coming to an end.

Jessie sat at my side, a set of keys dangling from her mouth.

After several minutes of Roland grovelling in the grass and nettles I called,

"I think Jessie has your keys Roland."

His head showed above the wall swearing unpleasantly about the dog and stamping over to grab the keys from her jaws, his suit now stained with grass and mud. Jessie was not a lover of men and certainly not this man. Dropping the keys, she snapped on Roland's hand causing him to scream more expletives as he danced around. I picked up the keys handing them to Roland and wished him a bonzer journey back to London.

"I've got them! I've got them! Move that damn thing!"

Angus took hold of Roland's lapels and, nose to nose, hissed, "Say please!"

Roland was suspended in Angus' grip six inches off the ground. "We don't expect to see you here again Laddie. Is that understood?"

"Yes! Yes!. Put me down!" he squealed.

"Please?"

"Please put me down."

Roland revved the engine as Angus moved the teleporter to let him roar off down the Glen road.

Plan B worked a treat gentlemen. Angus you were brilliant as the hired muscle, you scared the pants off him."

"I frightened myself." he laughed, "I didn't know I could enjoy myself being so nasty."

Tea and cake gentlemen?. A job well done. I cannot express my appreciation enough for your help."

"It's what friends are for Penny."

Alex took details of Roland's car saying he would ask his friend, a special constable in the tug o'war team, to put it on the police computer. Penny informed Mr Frobisher who advised that he would write to Roland with a warning that any further contact with Penny would be reported to the police as harassment and demanding money with menaces. He would also progress the sale with all due speed. Several weeks later, we would hear that Roland's hire car had been dumped near the Dover ferry terminal, implying he was heading for Luciana in Mallorca. He was also wanted by the police for failing to pay for the hire car and several drive offs at filling stations.

That evening after dinner and a celebratory damson gin I was sitting in the arm chair when Penny walked over and sat on my lap, her hands clasped in her lap and her head on my shoulder. I held her in an embrace and she quietly went to sleep.

"I love you dear Penny."

The next morning I slipped out of bed to make the tea. When I returned she was rousing and coming to her senses. "Why have I still got my clothes on?" she mused.

"You were on my lap and it was with great effort I got you into bed."

Taking a swig from her tea, she held the mug to her chest. "Last night did you say something to me when I was dropping off?"

"Nothing of any importance. I just whispered 'I love you dear Penny."

Penny had been shaken by the encounter with Roland.

"Do you know how many times you said no to Roland? You stood up to him really well. It took a lot of courage and determination to stand up to his bullying threats."

"That's the first time I have ever managed to do that. He always bullied and tormented me, twisting my arm, hurting me. He was cruel to me and our parents."

"I think yesterday has probably purged you of those years of anguish and fear."

"Can we go for a swim? I need to swim?" she pleaded.

"Naked or wet suit?"

"Naked. I need to cleanse myself totally. Get him out of my system."

"Sounds like South Pacific."

Penny looked at me quizzically.

"I'm gonna wash that man right out of my hair......"

RABBIT AND SPAR'RIB PIE

"Penny? We eat a lot of seafood and venison, so I was wondering about varying our diet with some different meat."

"That's fine by me, but it means a trip to the butchers in Ullapool or Inverness."

"I was thinking something free and nearer home. How do you feel about rabbit?"

"Well I don't like them eating my garden produce. I suppose I am OK with eating rabbit, but how do we go about it?"

"I asked Alex for his advice and he has lent us his air rifle. He says we can hide in the garden and shoot them from behind the wall."

"There's always lots of them early morning and evening, so worth a try I guess. Do you have a recipe in mind?"

"Two actually. When I had a week on the sporting estate at Kyllacky, we shot rabbit and turned them into a very tasty risotto. The other is rabbit and spar'rib pie.. We would have to get pork spare ribs from the butchers, but we could use pork belly or bacon. Are you any good at pastry?"

"Am I any good at pastry? Am I any good at pastry? She questioned indignantly, her voice rising to a crescendo implying a remonstration about her cooking ability.

"I will have you know my pastry is like grey cardboard!" she laughed.

"I'm ok with pastry. We had better practice our shooting so I will make some targets."

I raided the workshop, and over the next couple of days, cut out several sheet-metal rabbit-shaped targets, painting a white disc on the head. Morning and evening we observed the rabbits in the brae, placing the targets where they grazed. Our vantage point was a spot beyond the poly tunnel in the corner of the garden, hidden behind the wall, using it as a rest for the barrel. I built a wooden bench to perch on and a canvas covered frame to hide us from the rabbits and the elements. I learnt my lesson when I assumed wrongly that Penny could not cast a fly so enquired, "Did father teach you how to shoot?"

Penny was happy to receive instruction so we went through testing and adjusting the telescopic sight.

"When you are on target take a breath, hold it and squeeze the trigger gently."

She took to it like a duck to water and was soon bang on target hitting the white circles on the dummy rabbits. Now it was time for the real thing. Settling into our hide we watched and waited as several rabbits emerged, mainly young small ones so we bided our time waiting for the mature adults. We left our targets in place marking out a killing ground where we knew we could take effective shots. The rabbits were oblivious happily grazing around them. Penny picked her first rabbit but fizzed the pellet over its head into the grass bank causing it to jump up and turn round. Waiting until the rabbit was broadside and presenting the best possible shot, she squeezed the trigger and the rabbit rolled over. Penny was about to jump up and collect her prize, but I held her arm signalling with two fingers for a second. The rabbits seemed unperturbed by the loss of one of their number and eventually a second animal lolloped into the danger zone to be bowled over.

I showed Penny how to paunch and skin the first rabbit then remove the head and feet.

"It's a bit smelly. Very rabbitty, but I will have a go."

Having completed the task, we had two fresh carcasses.

"Well that was certainly a first for me. Makes a change from the chilled meat aisle in the supermarket, and quite rewarding." she commented.

Safely stored in the fridge we decided on rabbit risotto.

"I think it's your turn to teach me your foraging skills,

something to go in the risotto? Garlic and juniper perhaps, wild mushrooms?"

"Come on then. No time like the present." she declared grabbing her basket.

The brae provided the rabbit and we foraged along the burn around the silver birch, beech, oak, hazel and rowan trees. A low growing juniper provided fresh berries. Wild garlic was out of season, but on the stump of an old beech, I saw a cluster of yellow fungi.

"These any good?"

"Oh yes, oyster mushrooms, cut them off. Well spotted." I think Penny may well have led me to the spot allowing me find them.

"If the garlic is out of season, what about wild thyme?"

Penny immediately burst into song,

> And we'll all go together
> To pull wild mountain thyme
> All around the blooming heather
> Will you go, lassie, go?
> I will build my love a bower
> By yon clear and crystal fountain
> And on it, I will pile
> All the flowers of the mountain
> Will you go, lassie, go?
> And we'll all go together
> To pull wild mountain thyme
> All around the blooming heather
> Will you go, lassie, go?
> If my true love, he won't have me
> I will surely find another
> To pull wild mountain thyme
> All around the blooming heather
> Will you go, lassie, go?
> And we'll all go together
> To pull wild mountain thyme

> All around the blooming heather
> Will you go, lassie, go?

Our basket overflowed with more than our foraging.

"Penny?"

"Mmmmmm?" without lifting her eyes from her book.

"People here have been so kind and welcoming to this Sassenach, a complete stranger, so I would like to entertain them all to a meal. What do you think?"

"Splendid idea. That's eight of us."

"Plus Joe." I intervened.

"Nine then. We will not get them all in here?"

"Can we cook at the lodge do you think?"

"Yeees, yes we could. Menu?"

"Seafood starter, rabbit risotto, and rabbit pie, and something honey-based with your mead for pudding."

"I like it. When?"

"How about tomorrow?"

"Whaaaat?" she shrieked, then realised from the look on my face I was pulling her leg.

The following Friday was clear at the lodge and all gladly accepted the invitation, even Joe, who was quietly surprised and pleased to be included. He seldom ventured out now that he was on his own.

Sourcing seafood from our living larder was easy, but the pressure was on early morning sniping to get enough rabbits to fill the fridge. Vegetables from the poly tunnel completed our list of ingredients.

The evening was a delightful success, good friends enjoying good wine and good food, the rabbit dishes being a revelation. Sue declared they could be included on their game dinner events. Joe was a bit unsure of risotto being rather wary of foreign grub but tried and enjoyed it.

"Not had rabbit for years. Eilidh always did a good rabbit pie." He reminisced.

I made a speech thanking them all for their kindness, their acceptance and above all their friendship, offering a toast,

"Truly great friends are hard to find, difficult to leave, and impossible to forget."

Sue was wiping tears from her cheeks, Alex shook my hand and Joe just nodded asking for another glass of that honey stuff, "What do you call it? Mead?"

> And we'll all go together
> To pull wild mountain thyme
> All around the blooming heather
> Will you go, lassie, go?

HOLLYWOOD COMES TO TOWN

Dougal, the Postie, called for his customary morning cuppa, and breakfast if there was anything going.

"Any post for us Dougal?" Penny enquired eventually.

"Oh aye." replied Dougal, his mouth full of toast and homemade damson jam.

Dipping in his bag, he produced a posh looking envelope.

"Everyone's got one." he informed.

Dougal often knew most things by hanging about to see what was in your mail and then it would be on the jungle bagpipes. It was rumoured he even steamed letters open because he knew so much.

"Everyone on the estate, workers and residents have got one." He declared waving a wedge of envelopes in his hand. "It's from Mr Sinclair. Morag and Angus got the first one, you are second and now I am off to see everyone at the lodge."

"What does Mr Sinclair want Dougal?"

"I've nay idea I've not had a letter. Why not open it and read it." He enquired hoping for a bit of idle gossip.

Penny put the letter on the table, patted it and said, "Later." Much to Dougal's disappointment, realising his welcome was at an end.

As soon as his little red van had roared up the glen road, Penny opened the letter to find it was from Mr Sinclair's land agent. I was in suspense just watching her face as she read, smiled, "oohed, mmmmmm, Robert Louise Stevenson eh?", and finally declaring, "Hollywood is coming to town!"

I read the letter with my own ooohs and mmmms as Penny waited for my reaction."What do think?" she asked in a state of growing excitement.

"I think it will be great fun. Yes, great fun. Shall we both say 'yes'"

"I should say so."

Netflix planned to film part of a new series of Robert Louise Stevenson's, Kidnapped, the story of David Balfour disinherited, kidnapped and pursued with Alan Breck Stewart for the murder of Colin Roy of Glenure, "Red Fox", the notorious King's agent. The estate had agreed, for a fee, to filming on the estate land and asked all residents to give their co-operation to the project. All those concerned received invitations to a meeting at the lodge about the implications and extent of the filming.

It was scheduled for 11am followed by lunch and discussions

with specific individuals. Most were excited at the prospect and the possibility of being extras. There was much debate about their choice of dreamy film star. I remembered the 1971 version with Michael Caine playing Alan Breck.

By 1030 the ballroom was packed with participants taking coffee and biscuits. Peter Summers, Sinclair's Land Agent arrived the night before to host the meeting and now chaired the meeting with microphone and video projector. His introduction was basic, that the estate was cooperating with a film production unit who would be on the estate, weather permitting for about two weeks for location shots. Most of the filming would be elsewhere and in studios. He emphasised there would be some disruption to the estate and a little inconvenience, a lot of equipment vans, caravans etc and the lodge would be providing bed and breakfast. A catering contractor with a mobile kitchen would provide all meals, only requiring access to utilities. Peter then handed over to Hermione Wood, obviously a smart cookie from London who played a short video of the work her film company had done, including television adverts, documentaries and previous work for Netflix, BBC and so on. Clearly, a most professional and experienced set up.

Hermione gave a reprise of the story, involving the pursuit of David Balfour and Alan Breck Stewart across the moors by the Redcoats, landing on and leaving our shores by boat. The Lodge would feature some internal shots. Other locations had yet to be identified, but her two researchers would be staying for a few days looking at the moors, cottages, the beaches and so on. She emphasised that it would look like organised chaos with vans and coaches and horseboxes using the glen road and asked for our understanding. She offered a tasty morsel of extras in crowd scenes and backgrounds for which we would be dressed in period costume and make-up and, be well paid, but we had to expect a lot of standing around.

Her presentation and a buffet lunch were well received.

Hermione and her two researchers circulated the audience obviously getting a feel for those present and looking for any suitable extras. Angus MacLeòid was a prime target with his size and masses of red hair and beard receiving attention from the researchers and subsequently a chat with Hermione and a few snaps on their mobiles. The event certainly set the jungle bagpipes, drums and telegraphs alight with gossip and speculation.

The researchers stayed on for a few days identifying locations, taking lots of pictures and video. Alex was in great demand for expeditions over the moor, especially where they could get trucks over the ground to film. The lochan with the mare's tail was thought to be a most atmospheric location. They called to see Penny about a scene in the brae amongst the silver birch and asked if they could view the croft for internal shots, nothing spectacular just answering the door and a bedroom scene. Her paintings grabbed their attention because of the moody skies, but they were keen to know about the lady on the beach and where was the beach. We took them down to the jetty and along the path to our "surprise view" of the secret beach. They were in raptures, for beach scenes, embarking and disembarking from a rowing boat and the hill up to the mobile rock would be "absolutely fantastic" for the Red Coats to chase Balfour and Breck up it, or down it.

We got Landy out and took them along the top to the observation point where they identified the crossing point on the river and the rocky pools below where Balfour and Breck could hide while the Redcoats marched past.

River Eden gorge dropping to the beach

It was several weeks before we heard any more, until a schedule of filming arrived in the post with a request for one of us to help as a guide for the crews. On the appointed day, a crocodile of cars, lorries and vans crawled up the glen road to the lodge to be marshalled into place. Almost immediately, the catering crew got to work serving a hot meal, snacks and drinks all day. We walked up to see if we could help, but mainly we were just being nosy and we got a free meal. Some trailers were obvious by the signs on their doors, Costume, Makeup. Others were designated for actors but no star logos or names to give us a clue who the lead was, or even if he was coming. Breck was rumoured to be a well-known English actor and Balfour, a rising young star.

Balfour and Breck, Corstorphine, Edinburgh

A knock on the door revealed a wooden rowing boat on a trailer for delivery to the jetty and Doris was commandeered as safety boat. I was able to supply details about tides, submerged rocks and the depth of the channel in the river pool, as the scene would be Breck and Balfour descending the rocky pools to the beach and running for a boat to take them out of the bay. At the same time, Redcoats would descend the hill from mobile rock on foot and horseback shooting as they went, Red Fox observing from the top of mobile rock. The promontory would also be used as a landing place so we were asked to move our lobster pots.

It was all very exciting, especially when Breck and Balfour arrived at the croft to be entertained until called for their scene. Breck was particularly taken with the naked lady on the beach, assuming correctly it was Penny, in whom he also took a distinctly uncomfortable interest for this jealous bystander. Penny left him in no doubt that we were an item, but she was also thrilled by the attention. Balfour was a lot quieter showing less interest in the paintings and rehearsing his lines from the script. Of course, we took several selfies and received signed photographs.

All morning, equipment vans arrived with crew everywhere back and forth to the beach with cameras, lighting and sound equipment. Finally, all was set and the actors called to the beach for an explanation of their role, where they ran to, and where they boarded the boat.

The boat! Where is the other boatman? In the chaos, it had been missed that the second boatman was in bed at the lodge with Covid. The whole scene would be ruined. I was sitting in Doris, Seagull phutting, waiting the call to play my part as safety boat. The director ran along the path from the beach,

"We need an oarsman for this scene. Can you do it? All you have to do is row in to the shore and, when Breck and Balfour are aboard, row out. You know the bay."

I think I must have nodded a 'yes" because he then shouted, "Costume! Makeup! Get this man, er what's your name?"

"Charles."

"Get Charles some costume and makeup and a contract."

"Two ladies descended on me mopping my face with something and dragging me into a coat and floppy hat. "Keep the coat done up and stay seated so your clothes don't show on camera." A runner came up with a clipboard for me to sign a contract and my agreement to being in the movie.

"Mr Health and Safety then appeared, "Who is manning the safety boat. No filming without a safety boat." The director threw his arms in the air in desperation.

"I am manning the safety boat." declared Penny winking in my direction.

"Are you qualified?"

"I will have you know that I have sailed this bay and this boat since I was a child,"

"Yes but do you have qualifications?" pleaded Mr H&S.

"Inshore dinghy and day boat captain. I can show you the certificates later." retorted Penny whereupon Mr H&S capitulated.

Penny took over Doris as I sat in the rowing boat."I didn't know you had sailing certificates."

"I don't." she whispered but I had to say yes."

The rowing boat was about fifteen to eighteen feet long with three seating positions and two sets of oars. The other oarsman took the for'ard seat, and I took the middle position, facing Balfour and Breck on the rear.

Scenes tend to be filmed out of sequence and then stitched seamlessly together. Later in the day, they would film the pursuit of Breck and Balfour across the moor past mobile rock looking for the boat in the bay. When they get to the river, they would clamber down the rocky tree-lined gorge to the beach.

River Eden emerges on to the beach

A member of the crew climbed aboard Doris with a radio and Penny set off for the beach towing the rowing boat to the designated spot. The tide was right and the surface calm with a slight breeze. We sat there for a long time as they tested the lighting and sound and positioned the cameras.

All was ready. All I had to do was row to the beach and sit in the boat without turning round.

"That's a cut. Thank you Charles. Well done."

The cameras were re-positioned looking along the shore towards the river pool.

"Charles for the next scene, remain in the boat looking towards the river. Breck and Balfour will run along the shore, push the boat into the water, jump aboard and you row out. Ok? They will have dialogue so ignore what they say. Just row!"

"Sure. No problem."

"Action!"

Balfour and Breck ran along the shore to the sound of shots ringing out from the hill. A couple of Redcoats appeared by the river pool in hot pursuit. Balfour arrived first and the two pushed the boat away and jumped aboard. Breck screamed, "Row! Damn you man! Row for your life!"

Until now, Breck had been quiet and softly spoken, so I wasn't expecting, such fearsome dialogue when striving for realism, in character and embodying the role to such an extreme. The sign of a true professional instantly switching into his role, but it had the desired effect and adrenalin rush, as further shots rang out from the Redcoats stranded on the shore.

"Cut." Shouted the man with Penny, phutting over to take me in tow, clapping and smiling. "Well done. Well done. Excellent."

Back as his gentle self, Breck pointed out we now had to wait for LA. Apparently, the footage was streaming live to Los Angeles for approval, so we talked about fishing and our lives here, dining on lobster, scallops and salmon. Breck was a seafood aficionado bemoaning the catering on site and the hotel.

"Whereat Mr. Guppy chafes. So exceedingly that he with biting sarcasm informs his mother, in the confidential moments when he sups with her off a lobster and lettuce in the Old Street Road, that he is afraid the office is hardly good enough for swells.... Charles Dickens Bleak House." quoted Breck. What a wonderful memory actors must have.

I noted Penny's smiling face and discreet nods and winks. She was thinking the same as me.

"That's fine. Can the safety boat come in please?"

"They want a shot from the boat now as you row towards the bay."

Penny did as instructed, collecting a cinematographer with a handheld camera and a soundman with one of those fluffy microphones, seating them for'ard, Penny took them out, positioning behind the rowing boat.

"Ok, Charles. Keep your head down and row as fast as you can.

Breck and Balfour look for your ship waiting in the bay and occasional glances back at the shore. Ok?"

Thumbs up all round.

"Penny cut the engine please we will just float here."

"And action."

I rowed for all I was worth out to the entrance of the bay until I heard "Cut." with frantic waving from Doris. Thankfully, Doris phutted out to tow us back.

At the jetty Penny was desperate to take her chance,

"Breck. Would you and Balfour like to join Charles and I for a seafood supper at the croft. We have lobster, scallops, crab and if we beat the tide, possibly some razor clams?"

"Would I? Would I? My dear Penny, yes that would be splendid. May I bring the wine? I do need an early night as we have a very early start tomorrow morning. Would six be ok?"

Balfour politely declined, preferring to spend some time on his mobile to his girlfriend who was missing him.

I dashed to the shore with my carton of salt to pull a few razor clams from their holes, and a small bucket of mussels. With all the other items on our platter we only needed a couple of razor clams each. Returning, I raided our living larder for lobster, crab and scallops while Penny cleaned and tidied. I was soon back. The beauty of seafood is that it is easy and quick to cook and can be eaten cold. Our impromptu menu was; Moules marinière with cream, garlic and parsley, sautéed scallops, seafood platter of lobster and crab with lettuce and slices of Rob's smoked salmon.

Breck was deposited promptly by his chauffeur, a picture of elegance and cool sophistication in peach slacks, a silk shirt, deck shoes and the sleeves of a cashmere jumper draped over his shoulders. He walked up the drive sniffing wood smoke from the fire pit I constructed for outdoor cooking, mingled with the aroma of baking bread in the Dutch oven.

"We are al fresco if that is ok?"

"Absolutely. Splendid. What a view. Shall we start with champagne?" he enthused, handing over Vouvray and a Brut Champagne. There followed a meal fit for a king and a star of stage and screen who entertained us all evening with his theatrical tales.

"Penny, Charles, I have dined in restaurants all over the world, Michelin stars and all that but, I must say I have never enjoyed seafood so much, in your company, here in your croft, and the setting sun over the loch is magical. I am a man who thrives on publicity, my loyal fans, performing on stage and screen. It is my living, but if I wanted to escape from all that, then this is the place I would chose. My wonderful hosts, you are most fortunate to live your lives here."

Penny was effusive in her thanks for his appreciative comments and his company and desperate to ask her next question, shifting uneasily in her chair.

"What happens when the film is ready for release? Will there be a lot of publicity, a premiere and so on?"

"Oh yes, not a full-blown Hollywood extravaganza but there will be first nights in various locations, London obviously and possibly Edinburgh or Glasgow. Do you think you would like to come?"

"To quote a certain actor from earlier today. Would I? Would I? My dear Breck a team of wild horses would not stop me." she shrieked.

"Then Cinderella, you shall go to the ball, and you as well Captain Cook. Do you have a pen?"

Breck wrote a website on the back of his agent's card, "This website publishes in advance all the new releases and showbiz news. Keep an eye on it and when you see Kidnapped, ring my agent to remind him, and I will see you on the red carpet."

We lay in bed hoping that we had not given the star food poisoning and going over the day's events in detail.

"Well what a day! What an experience!" I exclaimed.

"A star is born." jested Penny.

"I wonder if I am likely to be mobbed by attractive groupies...." I pondered mischievously.

"They will have to get past me first dear! I want a ticket and a new dress for the premiere! What does the director say when they start filming a scene?"

" Lights! Camera! Action!" I replied.

"Oh director!"

WILTSHIRE

Gàradh Eden is a 'four day moor' meaning that, if there are sufficient grouse, the moor would accommodate four day's shooting of about two hundred brace per day. Weather and worm infestation can be fatal to young chicks if wet and cold weather strikes at the wrong time. Alex would spend all year tending the heather creating a patchy mosaic at different heights and maturity for cover and food. All this work would come together on the Glorious Twelfth of August the opening day of the grouse season. The first day was for Mr Sinclair's friends and family, the second was by invitation to other moor owners resulting in return invitations, and the remainder sold as let days to pay Alex's wages and the substantial costs.

After several fishing trips with his father, Joe, and the instruction from Mr Sinclair for me to load for him, Alex was more at ease with this English intruder. Moorland keepers are a breed apart, insular and isolated by the very nature of their work, often their only company being other gamekeepers, talking the same language of chick counts and worm infestation.

Even their clothing sets them apart, plus-four tweed breeks stopping half way down the shin before turning upwards forming a deep fold over long woollen socks and high-leg leather boots, the overlap stopping rain and muck going down the boot. A stranger visiting their lair at a remote moorland pub may fear earth had been invaded by extraterrestrial beings from the Planet Tweed. For all that, they are men of considerable mental and physical strength, tough, resilient, resourceful, resolute and oblivious to the harshest of elements. Alex's strength was regularly tested in the regional tug o'war team.

Hen Harrier

On one of our drives over the moors, I saw a bird get up out of the heather.

"Sparrow Hawk, Alex?"

"Och no. Hen harrier, she has a nest there."

"Is it right they nest close to other hen harriers?"

"Aye they do."

I was desperate to learn more but Alex was on his guard, wary of my interest or intentions.

"Dunna say anything about the harrier to anyone. It's my secret. I don't want antis or any busy-bodying do-gooders up here sticking their noses in. I am looking after the harriers. I do extra predator control in the nesting area, it's the foxes, stoats and weasels that takes the eggs and chicks, and the crows are as bad. When I have grouse chicks I leave day old hen chicks near the nests to feed the harriers and save them from taking grouse chicks."

"Is it working?"

"I think so. I have seen harriers fledging each year and I have plenty of grouse. You must have noticed as well all the waders, curlew, lapwing and golden plover."

Yes, I have on our walks up the brae. In fact now you mention I see them all round us."

"They have increased dramatically since I increased my predator control. There's enough room up here for all the birds if the moor is managed. Nae keeper. Nae grouse. Nae wading birds."

Alex showed me pictures on his mobile of the harrier in flight and on the nest and I could tell he was extremely proud.

"Don't worry Alex it's safe with me."

Conversation was not easy with Alex but I was gradually growing accustomed to his strong dialect and vocabulary, so we got by. I showed an interest in his work without appearing to pry and avoided topics that might raise his suspicion or lead to a distrust of me; Antis and persecution of raptors being two such hot topics.

"I hear you take groups of bird watchers on tours of the moor?"

"Aye I do. It's all income for the estate. Some struggle to see what they are looking for and I can keep them out of exclusion zones where the Golden Eagles nest. You know we have the right to roam up here so I am always suspicious of individuals and make a point of checking them out, let them know I have seen them. Sometimes they are photographers after pictures of protected birds on the nest, sometimes possibly egg collectors. Then we watch out for antis looking for an excuse to blame me for persecuting raptors. I know moors where they have planted poisoned carcases or birds that have been shot, so I have to be on my guard at all times. It's my job and my livelihood."

"I was on holiday on an estate where rabbits had been released providing food for the eagles. Apparently they hatch the chicks but there is insufficient food for them."

"Aye I know about that. They will take grouse and other mountain birds, white hares, rabbits and snakes. They also eat carrion."

"What about lambs?"

"We don't have many sheep up here and I think stories of them carrying off lambs are probably folk tales, a hare is about as much as they can carry. My job is to produce grouse for the shoot, I maintain their food source, the heather, and I control their predators, fox, stoat, weasel and carrion crow under licence. What I do protects all the ground nesting birds and rabbits and hare, providing more food for the eagles. Basically Charles, the fox and stoat pay the price up here to secure the future of the eagle."

After the four official shoot days, Alex assessed his remaining grouse stock to establish a viable ongoing population the moor could support. Alex and his neighbouring gamekeepers would shoot any excess and the birds sold to game dealers to grace the tables of high-end restaurants. Finally, I got the call, a precious invite indeed. Grouse shooting can be a dangerous pursuit with birds flying low between the butts and guns being peppered by their neighbours. One way to prevent this is to have two in a butt, one shooting forward and the other to the rear. I was paired with Big Jock, Mr Sinclair's usual loader who I had replaced. I am not sure if this pairing was intentional, Alex's perverse sense of humour perhaps, but Big Jock was indeed tall, slim and with a pleasant manner.

I think his greeting was something like, "Och ye wee Sassenach are ye?

Big Jock had a gift for talking but not conversation! He never stopped talking but you had no idea what he said, delivered at speed like the spitting of bullets from a machine gun, hence his nickname Tommy, as in tommy gun. Perhaps it was a ploy to lumber me with him for the day, a theory reinforced by the many keepers asking how we were getting on, with wry smiles and comments about donkeys hind legs. I did decipher one comment from Tommy that he could not understand a word Mr Sinclair said. It was a wonder St John got a word in edgeways.

The day was terrific, conducted in a stiff breeze with mature grouse speeding low over the heather. I took a brace home to Penny. Sadly, grouse is my least favourite game bird but it would have been an insult to refuse. Penny said she would make pate with juniper and damson gin, proving to be rather good, so good in fact; it went on the menu at the lodge.

In late September Alex, Isla, Penny and I packed Anja for a long trip to Eden House, the Sinclair home in the Cotswolds, nearly 600 miles and 11 hours solid, if we were lucky with the traffic. Stowed in the boot was a cool-box crammed with a live lobster, scallops, razor clams fillets of Pollock, Penny's grouse pate and vacuum-packed fillets of venison. Penny shared the driving, as Alex and Isla were not so keen, especially when it came to "blue roads," the motorways. Life was far too fast for them.

In the early evening, we arrived at their Cotswold mansion built with mellow weathered creamy limestone and stone roof tiles all hewn from local quarries. The mansion stood on a huge plot surrounded by matching stone walls, accessed by black gold-tipped iron gates opening on to a wide expanse of gravel, beautiful lawns and flower beds. A strange square tower about three stories high stood isolated among the lawns. A large oak door led to an empty interior, the walls rising to a line of windows and vents topped with a tile roof. Closer examination of the room revealed a line of fireplaces around the base of the walls. It was an ancient kitchen or cookhouse and the blackened walls evidenced the smoke from the open fires to the vents above. Behind the cookhouse stood a beautiful chapel, complete with spire and graveyard, and beyond, a walled garden.

The house interior was all you would expect and more, luxurious, comfortable and extravagant. Our accommodation was a suite of rooms in the converted stable and coach house. A quick shower and we were ready for champers and hors d'oeuvre including some of Penny's grouse pate. This is the life. St John and Samantha were the most gracious and welcoming hosts. I think Penny and I were more comfortable in these surroundings and their presence, unrestricted by employee deference and having considerable experience of the world beyond the Scottish border.

When I awoke, the next morning madam was luxuriating in a huge copper bath. I find this modern trend of bathing in a bedroom very strange and rather uncomfortable, an intrusion on one's privacy, especially if one suffers from flatulence. Even more disconcerting was a bijou hotel I stayed in, converted from a convent and incorporating the "Chapel Suite." It was comfortable and luxurious with a lounge area moving into a bed zone, a shallow partition hid the huge copper bathtub and higher up in the altar section, a walk-in shower and toilet. All open plan. No wonder my American friend woke in the night to find two Nuns sitting on the bed and one hovering above him. He was adamant they were ghosts but we put it down to an excess of Famous Grouse.

Anyway, beggars cannot be choosers and waste not, want not, as Penny stepped out I stepped into the perfumed foamy water. Penny had done some investigative girl-talk establishing Samantha was from a wealthy Home Counties family, Cheltenham Ladies College, then University College London to qualify as a pharmacist to join father's small chain of shops, later bought out by a national conglomerate. She bred Highland Ponies on the estate.

"Very informative Dr Watson."

After buffet breakfast in the dining room, Samantha whisked the girls off on a tour of the Cotswolds and lunch at the Lygon Arms in Broadway, sharing the barbecue beef platter. Penny said there was a lot of fish and seafood on the menu but we have so much of that at home she wanted beef.

Alex was scheduled for an estate-planning meeting with St John so I was given a seven foot split cane rod and box of trout flies to entertain myself on the chalk stream in the garden. It was a glorious back yard, manicured lawns running down to the stream and following its course through a gate into the adjoining fields, a path mown along the bank. It was a crystal-clear chalk stream fast flowing with a gritty stone bed supporting masses of weed vibrating and pulsating in the current. I observed brown trout resting on the bed in channels between the weed, gently flexing their tails and bodies to maintain their position, facing upstream, awaiting a passing fly or nymph. A flash of electric blue shot downstream to rest on his fishing perch before arrowing into the stream and returning with a small fish. The riverbank was stacked with bird and insect life.

Adjacent to the field gate was a most unusual construction. For want of a better word, it was a tree house but on a grand scale, about ten feet square built on a dozen telegraph poles, walls planked with silver-grey waney edge oak boards, a thatched roof with a peacock as its crowning glory standing on the ridge. Access was via an iron spiral staircase to a heavily padlocked door.

I disturbed several trout with my heavy handed casting

splashing the fly onto the surface film. Progressing upstream, I eventually managed a cast on the nose of a trout that rose swiftly, white mouth gaping, to grab the fly then instantly spitting it back at me before disappearing into the weeds. At least I deceived a fish into taking the fly.

In the afternoon, Alex took me to meet the estate gamekeeper Will Turner, and a guided tour of the shoot. The estate was immaculate, nothing out of place, gates, fences and hedges maintained, the shooting pegs clearly numbered facing the rolling hills of the downs, carpeted in acres of stubble following the grain harvest. Alex and Will are both gamekeepers, but miles apart in distance, language, dress and their respective roles.

We arrived back at the house for tea just as Samantha's Range Rover disgorged the girls and numerous carrier bags. Will and his wife joined us for dinner where conversation was shooting and shopping in equal measure. St John was keen to ensure all was ready for tomorrow's shoot, briefing us on the guests and plans for the day. The ladies discussed fashions in readiness for the 150 boutiques at Bicester Village shopping destination.

Over a quiet whisky, I asked about the tree house.

"Father's retreat. Whenever nuclear war loomed in the form of mother exploding in a mushroom cloud, that is where he ran for cover. Originally it had a trap door and a retractable ladder to stop mother climbing up to him. To be fair he used it as a quiet place away from work, where he was able to smoke his pipe, drink brandy, read his paper, Times crossword, tie flies and observe the nature around him. Mother often said he had a woman up there. 'Chance would be a fine thing' he would say."

"I assume Eden House is named after the lodge Gàradh Eden?"

"Now that is a little complicated. Has Penny told you about the lodge in the seventies?"

"The army took it over I believe as part of Operation Candid."

"Yes indeed they did. Her father seconded the lodge and the croft for the MOD during the Cold War as a hideout for Adam and

Eve."

"Adam and Eve?"

"Yes code words for the Queen and Prince Phillip, so they would be hidden in the Garden of Eden if the Russians started a war. The lodge was renamed Gàradh Eden and the croft was a sort of listening and security post guarding the road and the jetty. In an emergency, tenders from Navy ships, the Royal Yacht etc could drop supplies and passengers at Traigh Parras, Paradise Beach on the River Eden. The lodge and croft were erased from maps and even the name of the river was changed to confuse the Ruskies. The top room in the tower was turned into a television studio for the Queen to broadcast to the nation, keep morale up and so on. Never came to anything of course, and I don't think Adam and Eve ever paid a visit, but we did get the lodge refurbished just in case, plus a rental, and we carried on shooting.

Shoot and shopping day dawned with Alex and I reporting to the big house to meet the other guests for breakfast. The six guns, immaculately turned out in tweed suits, were mainly city men, each with a chauffeur-loader, taking breakfast in a separate dining room.

We drew silver tabs from a leather pouch to find our peg number underneath, followed by a safety briefing and we were off. After introductions to our loaders, chosen from estate workers, Alex and I jumped aboard the gun bus. We shot double guns, as if on the grouse moor, as clouds of French Partridge and an occasional covey of English Partridges, sailed towards us on the wind to be mopped up by a team of pickers-up working an array of Spaniels and Labradors. Glorious sport.

Lunch was nibbles in the field at a purpose built hospitality area on the wooded banks of a small lake, an open-sided timber log cabin with fire pits on the table and comfortable seating. Wirework sculptures of deer, boxing hares and a horse dotted the lake edges as we dined on smoked salmon, pie, rare beef, salads and breads, washed down with rare wines and champers.

The guests knew each other so there was a lot of talk about politics and finance. Alex looked the odd one out in his moorland plus-fours but also attracted the attention of several grouse shooters. In a way, I was the odd one out, even though I looked the part, I did not have an estate nor vast wealth and it was difficult to explain who I was and what I did; film extra, author, retired copper, loader, lobster fisher, scallop diver, Rabbie Burns orator and haggis slayer. I was an enigma, an inscrutable and mysterious person indeed.

After the shoot, we retired to the big house for tea and cake attended by two happy smiley ladies arming several designer brand carriers. Penny stunned the room with her entrance and I could feel the jealousy as she plonked a smiley kiss on my cheek. She was a happy bunny. Unbeknown to the guns I was to be the entertainment at dinner.

Penny was desperate to show me her purchases funded from our tips. I was required to sit on a chair at the side of the catwalk, her iPhone providing the music as she disappeared into the bedroom. Reappearing in the same clothes, but pointing at her Jimmy Choo shoes, strutting her stuff and returning to the bedroom. Her hand appeared round the doorjamb, slowly followed by an arm and a gradual revealing of a super glamorous, revealing gown, by "Nadine Merabi!" she declared, shiny slinky shimmery gold, and rather revealing, her tanned leg peeking out from a long slit in the side. She looked a million dollars. "This is for our premiere she declared."

"Absolutely fabulous darling!"

Beaming, she trotted back to the bedroom, indicating with a raised hand that I remain seated.

I thought there would be a repeat performance, as the hand appeared again followed by the arm and a gradual revealing of nearly all of Penny's tanned body. I watched open-mouthed as she slinked towards me smiling and assessing the impact.

"Is it the queen's new clothes?" Was not the response she

anticipated.

"Queen's new clothes?" she exclaimed.

"You know, 'The queen is in the all together and all together as naked as the day she was born,' an invisible set of clothing for the king's parade."

"I'm not naked Charles!" Pointing to her matching bra and pant set.

"Ah! New knickers!"

As a man, I lack the knowledge and vocabulary to describe adequately her lingerie but it was neither cheap, tawdry nor tarty. "Au contraire Rodney" to quote Del Boy Trotter, it was classy, elegant, colourful, tasteful and probably expensive.

"Knickers? Knickers! I'll have you know this is luxury designer lingerie by Kiki de Montparnasse darling."

The name was lost on me as anything outside of Marks and Spencer is a completely new world.

"Are you going to take it off?" she asked more softly.

"I'm not wearing it." I teased.

"Charles! You know what I mean." she chided seductively.

"Oh well duty calls……………."

We were nearly late for dinner, Penny in her black cocktail dress and Jimmy Choos and myself in Highland dress. Yes, it was another Burns supper and I have to say I was getting rather tired of haggis, but luckily, it was only a starter to get things going with a swing.

The next morning was our long trek back north. It was dark when I dropped Penny at the Croft to boil the kettle while I took Alex and Isla home. As I walked to the front door, I was welcomed by the flickering of a roaring log fire heating the back boiler and taking the chill off the room.

"Tea in bed?" Penny asked.

"Yes please."

It was good to be home.

THE PREMIERE

Breck was true to his word. A very excited Postie arrived at the cottage, horn pipping, ready for his tea, toast and gossip. On this occasion, he was more interested in the gossip,

"You have a letter frae London, the film company." he informed.

The estate and those of us who played extras had been the talk of the locality, interviews with local papers, local radio and BBC Highlands and Islands, but we remained very minor celebrities. The film company had been prompt in sending cheques for my extra role, Penny's safety boat and even a fee for the hire of Doris.

"They have some at the lodge as well," exclaimed the excited Dougal.

Penny slipped her butter knife under the envelope seal slitting it open and peeping inside.

"Oh yes. We were expecting these. Weren't we Charles?"

Penny placed the letter on the table secured beneath a pot of honey. Dougal was devastated by the anti-climax, unable to tell them at the lodge about the contents of their letters.

As soon as he left, Penny dived into the envelope to find a letter from Breck and two tickets for the premiere in Edinburgh. Not just the premiere but an invite to meet for pictures on the red carpet and the after-film party.

"I told you I needed a new dress for the premiere." she whooped.

Sue, Morag and Angus also had tickets but in spite of his role as an extra, Angus was not keen. "I dinna like the city and all those people, and I have the cows to milk." So, Sue, Morag, Penny and myself set off on a five hour journey to Edinburgh for a weekend of celebrity and shopping. It was an early start, allowing time for booking in at the Royal Scots Club and sightseeing, followed by afternoon tea at The Dome, formerly The Commercial Bank Of Scotland building, now a renowned and resplendent venue.

Royal Scots Club Edinburgh

The following morning the ladies hit the shops and I wandered along Princes Street trying to recall the kilt shop I visited as a child. Mother, foolishly, said if I could find my name on the lists of family and clan associations, I could have a kilt. Sure enough, I found my Irish grandfather's name of Whyte.

My great affection was for my English grandfather born in 1884, who worked as a horse driver in a Derbyshire coalmine from the age of thirteen. At seventeen, he signed up for the 2nd Battalion Royal Scots as the Regiment embarking for a nine year tour in India. I have often wondered at the extreme contrast from the dark depressing depths of a coalmine to the sights, sounds and smells of India. He may have enjoyed his time there as a good footballer playing for the Royal Scots Minto Rovers 1906-1907 -

India's Football Champions. He was called up for WW1 and went to France with the British Expeditionary Force in 1914, possibly wounded, and returned to serve in the 3rd Battalion stationed at Edinburgh Castle.

India's Football Champions: The Royal Scots.

I decided to visit the regimental museum at the castle and enquire about the appropriate tartan for the Royal Scots. Standing on the ramparts next to Mons Meg, I took a few minutes to reflect on my grandfather and my return over a century later.

I had decided that my place in my new community was now permanent, meriting a kilt of my own, so armed with the new tartan information; I quickened my pace to the kilt makers. On my return to our room at the Royal Scots Club, I found the bed littered with designer carrier bags. The "premiere" dress hung on the wardrobe door, the Kiki De Montparnasse lingerie at its side on a chair and the Jimmy Choos beneath. Madame was relaxing in the bath with a glass of bubbly.

"Hello celebrity. Had a good day?"

"Mmmmmm." she replied, water and bubbles up to her neck,

eyes closed, sipping her bubbly.

"Want your back scrubbing?"

"Mmmmmm please."

The UK premiere was at the Edinburgh Film Festival with arrivals on the red carpet from 6 to 630pm, to start at 7pm after a champagne reception for the "celebrities." All the ladies invaded our room to get ready so I was enveloped in hot air and hormones as the excitement mounted. I was banished to the bathroom to wash up and kilt up, knocking on the door to see if it was safe to enter the bedroom.

A taxi swept us to the cinema with instructions to deposit us at the end of the carpet at 605pm. We were amongst the first to arrive so the gathering crowds took great interest trying to identify us. I don't think anyone recognised us, no one shouted our names and there were no requests for autographs or selfies. Not surprising really but a paparazzi did get a few snaps as we paused and poised in front of the advertising boards. We lingered as long as we dare, smiling and waving in our moments of fame before entering the foyer. Numerous unknowns followed us but at 640pm there were loud screams and shouts at the arrival of Balfour with his girlfriend on his arm. We had to enquire as to the girlfriend, to be informed she was a model appearing in a television reality romance on a desert island show. I never understood Big Brother and all the subsequent spin-offs so it was all a mystery to me. She was certainly lapping up the attention with a massive smile bursting from her botoxed pumped up lips.

"I hope you are not getting too excited by her darling."

"With nails that long she would be no good chopping logs, would she?"

Breck was obviously going to make a dramatic entrance as the star of the movie and, on cue, a white Rolls Royce appeared and out stepped our Breck, in full Highland dress smiling and waving and working his audience and fans. He saw Penny watching from the entrance and immediately strode over to take her hand, gesturing me to follow and we stood together in front of a blitz of camera flashes, photographers calling for Breck to look their way. Finally Breck gestured us away and he had one last blast with the cameras and stepped inside. He was genuinely pleased to see us and started introducing us to a plethora of film people, as his friends and fellow actors.

The bell rang for us to take our seats and we joined Sue and Morag with great excitement and anticipation. It was hard not to shout out "Look that's such and such a location!" and when I appeared in the boat, I thought they might stand up whistling and hollering. It was a very brief glimpse of my acting abilities with my face barely visible. We watched the credits to the very end and sure enough, we caught sight of our names in the extras and safety boat. Fame at last. Not that I wanted fame and of course no mention would be made to the next party of visiting Americans.

We chosen few were shepherded to the function room adjoining the auditorium for nibbles and more champagne, mixing with who knows whom from the film world. Penny looked a million dollars in her long gold gown, a slender leg peeping through a slit, and her gloriously white smile beaming through her tanned complexion.

Breck spent some time with us but he had a job to do with producers and directors and film moguls, but his interest in us generated an interest with others in the room keen to know who we were and what we did. I only made a slight reference to being an author with Penny my editor and publisher, which seemed to satisfy their desire for information.

It was a fantastic evening and a wonderful, unique experience contrasting hugely with our long drive home the next morning.

BOOK ENDS

Pip, peep, peep, pip!

"That sounds like Dougal. I wonder what tasty morsels of gossip he has for us today."

Sure enough, it was Dougal the Postie, and in he walked taking his usual seat at the kitchen table.

"Have you time for tea and perhaps a slice of toast or do you have urgent business up the glen today?"

"Och no, plenty of time. Aye tea and toast would be fine."

"Damson jam or whisky marmalade?"

"You do know the way to a Postie's heart. Aye the marmalade would be fine."

Dougal was managing director and head broadcaster of the jungle bagpipes network knowing everything from the price of sheep at market to who is rumoured to be sleeping with whom.

"Anything happening hereabouts Dougal?"

"Och nay it's certainly been a wee bit dead since the film crew left. I see you have pictures of Breck and Balfour on the sideboard."

"Did you know Charles was called up last minute to row the boat and I used Doris as safety boat."

"No! No! I didn't ken that at all."

"Did you have any other reason for calling, apart from tea and toast?"

"Oh aye there's a letter." he said spitting crumbs while munching through half a slice of toast."

"It's frae London." He crumbed.

"How fascinating Dougal. Any idea who from?"

"Aye a publisher, I think."

"Could be important Charles couldn't it, you being a renowned author?"

"Yes indeed Penny."

"Are you delivering it today Dougal?"

"Aye it's here in my bag." Slowly reaching in to extract the letter. Penny placed it on the sideboard.

"Are ye no going to open it then?" he enquired, sensing a bit of news to pass on at his next tea spot.

"Oh not yet. Probably not very important at all. Have you done with your pots Dougal, so I can finish washing up? Brush your crumbs off outside Dougal please. I have just vacuumed."

Dougal was still cramming the last of his toast, heavily spread with butter and whisky marmalade, while swilling it down with half a mug of tea. He stood up slowly folding his arms in a vain attempt to trap the toast debris scattered over his blue uniform.

"Bye Dougal. See you again soon."

"Aye, see you soon. Thanks for the tea and toast."

"Penny you are a proper little minx tormenting poor Dougal like that. He will now think the letter contains a great secret, a matter of great interest and importance."

"I know. He may be right Charles."

My curiosity was now aroused but I was not going to rise to the bait. This trout was staying firmly on the riverbed.

It is not surprising for Penny to get a letter from her old publishing company, her friend works there, she had a pension from them, so possibly just financial administration.

Penny gathered the letter and a silver opener with a thistle handle mounted with an Amethyst. Her eyes remained on me noting my reaction as she slid the blade slowly along the crease ending with a flourish and returning the knife to the sideboard.

Removing the contents slowly, almost seductively, Penny unfolded the single sheet. I could see it was an A4 typed document but the text was indecipherable. The minx read the letter slowly and deliberately, but not aloud, apart from an odd "Oh" or "Mmm", sometimes smiling and sometimes with eyebrows raised.

I had a feeling this was all to do with my authored works and me. Penny was toying with me, casting a yellow drake mayfly on my nose, teasing me to snap at the fly so she could reel me in. She was desperate for me to make some comment.

"Come on Penny spill the beans."

I was hooked.

"You know I have been reading your novels?"

I nodded, responding with a long drawn out questioning, "Yeeeesss?"

"Well I sent them to my friend at my old publishers with my review."

She paused.

"And?"

"She agrees with my review." pausing again.

Another long, drawn out questioning, "Yeeeesss?"

"They don't like them Charles." She paused less briefly this time as my eyes sank in disappointment, "They absolutely love them! They love the stories and your descriptive style of writing, but to be commercial they require professional editing. They see great potential as books and eBooks, backed by their marketing and the possibility of TV or even film rights!"

"That would be rather good now that I am an established film star. Which novels are they interested in?"

"The Hidden Glen and Penny from heaven. Delia Archer the editor adores Boy from the Building Site, saying it is a brilliant idea, a unique story with great appeal to a younger audience especially as a children's TV serial. She also says how good your descriptive writing is, and she could see the scenes and the feelings around them. The three together will make you high profile boosting interest in Shaggy Dog Stories.

Penny rushed over to give me a huge hug, handing me the letter.

I skim read it quickly as Penny waited on tenterhooks for my reaction. Then I read it slowly and deliberate looking for the catch and testing her patience.

"They are offering me an advance on each one. Is it a good deal?"

"Too right it is. They want you and are prepared to pay well. Of course, they hope to make a bundle on publishing rights."

"Will I be famous? Will I be a celebrity? Will I have go on all those silly celebrity quiz or cooking shows? More importantly, will I become a sex object constantly beating off a string of young women with long nails and botox lips?"

I noticed Penny smiling and shaking her head.

"Will I have to leave the Croft?" I asked more sombrely.

"Will I lose you in the rush to literary stardom? The Booker Prize perhaps?"

Penny's eyebrows raised in disbelief.

"I'm not doing Strictly. Nor eating bugs in a jungle with Ant and Dec."

"I cannot stand yawpy TV with a load of so called celebrities I've never heard of. Yeah sounds good. Where do I sign?"

Penny pushed past me but was immediately entangled in an embrace."

"As if I would want to leave the Croft or my dear Penny."

"Publish and be damned," she said, "and we will take whatever comes. We are strong enough to deal with anything, aren't we? We don't have to leave the Croft it will always be our retreat, our hideaway to escape from the mad rushing crowds."

"If the worst came to the worst we could employ Angus as bodyguard scooping up the paparazzi with his teleporter."

"We don't need the money do we? Or, the fan worship? The publicity? All we need is each other and our lifestyle, don't we?"

"The proceeds would benefit the family and we could support good causes as well."

"As long as we are together"

"Charles please sit in the armchair. Not that one. This one. Close your eyes."

I sensed Penny leaving the room and then returning somewhere between my chair and the fireplace.

"Keep them shut."

I sensed her stepping aside, "Now you can open your eyes."

I looked straight at Penny but saw nothing of such interest that it merited a reveal as if it was The Repair Shop. Penny had a huge smile and was looking and nodding towards the fireplace.

"That's me. That's me. That's my portrait." I shouted jumping to my feet. "Oh, you clever, wonderful girl. That's. That's. Beautiful!"

Wiping the mistiness from my eyes, I hugged Penny rocking from side to side in a warm embrace.

"When you are on the celebrity treadmill beating off all those young female fans, I will always have this picture of you won't I? And if you don't come back I can use it as a dart board."

More hugs and kisses as Penny whispered in my ear, "There's more." Her eyes led me to the paintings above the fireplace, the once empty space now filled with my portrait. I looked and looked but my eyes were too blind to see.

"Give me those spectacles to clean and wipe your eyes."

"Now look again." she instructed glancing to the side of my portrait and the painting of the naked woman on the beach.

"Tràigh Pàrras, Paradise Beach. My paradise, but now our paradise."

I scanned it quickly and then I saw it! Well not an 'it', but a second person, a man, me, naked walking at her side.

Penny stood at my side, her arm round me and her hand resting on my shoulder.

"We will always be on our beach together."

"This is BBC Radio Cambridgeshire, traffic report. We are just getting reports of a major pile up on the A1M at junction seventeen, northbound. North and southbound carriageways are blocked."

"Chas! Chas! Did you hear that? The A1M is blocked at Peterborough!"

As the BBC traffic news repeated the message, I searched Anja's satnav for an alternative route home from our Norfolk holiday, as the red congestion spider on the satnav extended its legs, creeping along the A47 from Peterborough towards us.

"Turn right at the next roundabout. We will go across country through The Fens to Spalding and Newark and then back home."

Parras air chall.

Paradise lost.

Address to a Haggis - Robert Burns

Fair fa' your honest, sonsie face,
Great Chieftain o' the Puddin-race!
Aboon them a' ye tak your place,
Painch, tripe, or thairm:
Weel are ye wordy of a *grace*
As lang 's my arm.

The groaning trencher there ye fill,
Your hurdies like a distant hill,
Your *pin* wad help to mend a mill
In time o' need,
While thro' your pores the dews distil
Like amber bead.

His knife see Rustic-labour dight,
An' cut ye up wi' ready slight,
Trenching your gushing entrails bright,
Like onie ditch;
And then, O what a glorious sight,
Warm-reekin, rich!

Then, horn for horn, they stretch an' strive:
Deil tak the hindmost, on they drive,
Till a' their weel-swall'd kytes belyve
Are bent like drums;
Then auld Guidman, maist like to rive,
Bethankit hums.

Is there that owre his French *ragout*,
Or *olio* that wad staw a sow,
Or *fricassee* wad mak her spew
Wi' perfect sconner,
Looks down wi' sneering, scornfu' view
On sic a dinner?

Poor devil! see him owre his trash,
As feckless as a wither'd rash,
His spindle shank a guid whip-lash,

His nieve a nit;
Thro' bluidy flood or field to dash,
O how unfit!

But mark the Rustic, *haggis-fed*,
The trembling earth resounds his tread,
Clap in his walie nieve a blade,
He'll make it whissle;
An' legs, an' arms, an' heads will sned,
Like taps o' thrissle.

Ye Pow'rs wha mak mankind your care,
And dish them out their bill o' fare,
Auld Scotland wants nae skinking ware
That jaups in luggies;
But, if ye wish her gratefu' prayer,
Gie her a *Haggis*!

Address to a Haggis Translation

Good luck to you and your honest, plump face,
Great chieftain of the sausage race!
Above them all you take your place,
Stomach, tripe, or intestines:
Well are you worthy of a grace
As long as my arm.

The groaning trencher there you fill,
Your buttocks like a distant hill,
Your pin would help to mend a mill
In time of need,
While through your pores the dews distill
Like amber bead.

His knife see rustic Labour wipe,
And cut you up with ready slight,
Trenching your gushing entrails bright,
Like any ditch;
And then, O what a glorious sight,
Warm steaming, rich!

Then spoon for spoon, the stretch and strive:
Devil take the hindmost, on they drive,
Till all their well swollen bellies by-and-by
Are bent like drums;

Then old head of the table, most like to burst,
'The grace!' hums.

Is there that over his French ragout,
Or olio that would sicken a sow,
Or fricassee would make her vomit
With perfect disgust,
Looks down with sneering, scornful view
On such a dinner?

Poor devil! see him over his trash,
As feeble as a withered rush,
His thin legs a good whip-lash,
His fist a nut;
Through bloody flood or field to dash,
O how unfit.

But mark the Rustic, haggis-fed,
The trembling earth resounds his tread,
Clap in his ample fist a blade,
He'll make it whistle;
And legs, and arms, and heads will cut off
Like the heads of thistles.

You powers, who make mankind your care,
And dish them out their bill of fare,
Old Scotland wants no watery stuff,
That splashes in small wooden dishes;
But if you wish her grateful prayer,
Give her [Scotland] a Haggis!

ACKNOWLEDGEMENT

Photograph attributions

Angel of the North   By Barly.. - https://www.flickr.com/photos/red-mandy/6150534524/, CC BY 2.0, https://commons.wikimedia.org/w/index.php?curid=115814369

Kyllaky House   Author

Beach Road Salthouse   Author

Atom Bombs   Public domain

Royal Yacht   By Ben Salter from Wales - farewell BrittaniaUploaded by Oxyman, CC BY 2.0, https://commons.wikimedia.org/w/index.php?curid=22457043

Forth Bridges   By M J Richardson, CC BY-SA 2.0, https://commons.wikimedia.org/w/index.php?curid=71199033

The Kelpies   By © User:Colin / Wikimedia Commons, CC BY-SA 4.0,   https://commons.wikimedia.org/w/index.php?curid=46446772

River Orchy   Author

Ganavan Sands   © Copyright Steve Houldsworth and licensed for reuse under this Creative Commons Licence

Bonnie Prince Charlie Statue Derby   Bonnie Prince Charlie Statue, Derby Bonnie Prince Charlie cc-by-sa/2.0 - © Tony Bacon

- geograph.org.uk/p/1685934

Corrour Station © Thomas Nugent cc-by-sa/2.0 :: Geograph Britain and Ireland

The Hidden Glen by the author

River Shiel Jane Ball

The Jacobite "The Jacobite" departs from Mallaig cc-by-sa/2.0 - © John Lucas - geograph.org.uk/p/879905

River Morar Author

A Chruach © Copyright Colin Park and licensed for reuse under this Creative Commons Licence geograph.org.uk/p/5613977.

Old Forge Inverie The Old Forge Knoydart cc-by-sa/2.0 - © John Watson - geograph.org.uk/p/931336

Community Shop Inverie Knoydart Foundation

Prince's Cairn The Prince's Cairn, Loch nan Uamh cc-by-sa/2.0 - © Gordon Brown - geograph.org.uk/p/2974817

Glenfinnan Monument Loch Shiel from Glenfinnan viewpoint cc-by-sa/2.0 - © Norrie Adamson - geograph.org.uk/p/204100

Applecross sign Jane Ball

Applecross © Copyright Julian Paren and licensed for reuse under this Creative Commons Licence.

Loch Maree Jerry Sharp Geograph

Keanchulish House © Copyright Ike Gibson and licensed for reuse under this Creative Commons

Licence.

Pollock   By © Citron, CC BY-SA 3.0, https://commons.wikimedia.org/w/index.php?curid=24350181

Dutch Oven   https://belltent.co.uk/products/premium-cast-iron-dutch-oven-12-inch-6-quart

Highland Cattle on beach © Copyright Calum McRoberts and licensed for reuse under this Creative Commons Licence.

River Canaird on the run into the Doire an Fhudair gorge   © Copyright ian shiell and licensed for reuse under this Creative Commons Licence.

Mobile Rock   © Copyright Richard Webb and licensed for reuse under this Creative Commons Licence.

Langwell Lodge Strath Canaird   © Copyright Alan Reid and licensed for reuse under this Creative Commons Licence.

Prestwold Hall Leicestershire Author

Prestwold Hall Leicestershire Author

Poster Kaylilcorey

Sea trout   Public domain Copyright by: Wolfgang Striewski www.meerforellen.info

Robert Burns, 1759 – 1796 Scottish National Portrait Gallery Collection by Alexander Nasmyth (1758–1840) The official position taken by the Wikimedia Foundation is that *"faithful reproductions of two-dimensional public domain works of art are public domain"*. This photographic reproduction is therefore also considered to be in the public domain in the United States.

Haggis   Autorstwa Lordvolom1 - Praca własna, CC BY-SA 4.0, https://commons.wikimedia.org/w/index.php?

curid=46371629

Lobster pot By EinirWOwen - Own work, CC BY-SA 4.0, https://commons.wikimedia.org/w/index.php?curid=107093514

Lobster By Bart Braun - Own work, Public Domain, https://commons.wikimedia.org/w/index.php?curid=4425087

Doris https://woodenships.co.uk/contact/ Dartmouth Devon

Highland Games Weight throw GNU Free Documentation License,

Seagull outboard Creative Commons CC0 1.0 Universal Public Domain Dedication.

Doris bean an locha

Beauly Square Creative Commons Attribution-Share Alike 3.0 Unported license.Attribution: Alan Jamieson

Campbells This file is licensed under the Creative Commons Attribution-Share Alike 4.0 International license.

Scallop Rachael Norris and Marina Freudzon / Mayscallop at en.wikipedia, Public domain, via Wikimedia Commons

Landy By Dennis Elzinga - Land Rover Lightweight, CC BY 2.0, https://commons.wikimedia.org/w/index.php?curid=38639059

Falls of Falloch © Copyright Graeme Smith and licensed for reuse under this Creative Commons Licence.

Crane Fly Author

Air raid siren Dominic Winter Auctions

WB400 receiver Ringbell.co.uk

Twenty Six Years Reminiscences of Grouse Moors Adams. Public domain

Red Grouse   By MPF - Own work, CC BY-SA 3.0, https://commons.wikimedia.org/w/index.php?curid=47878712

Mouse fly   Fish4flies

Kidnapped book   From Booksalvation (Manchester, United Kingdom)

Gorge   © Copyright ian shiell and licensed for reuse under this Creative Commons Licence.

Kidnapped Statue   By Kim Traynor - Own work, CC BY 3.0, https://commons.wikimedia.org/w/index.php?curid=12958320

Emergence from the chasm for River Canaird   For NC1901 And © Copyright ian shiell and licensed for reuse under this Creative Commons Licence.

Hen Harrier   Isle of Man Government, CC BY 2.0 <https://creativecommons.org/licenses/by/2.0>, via Wikimedia Commons

Eagle exclusion zone on River Canaird near Ullapool   © Copyright ian shiell and licensed for reuse under this Creative Commons Licence.

Royal Scots Club By Rwatson1955, CC BY-SA 4.0, https://en.wikipedia.org/w/index.php?curid=61812603

Royal Scots football champions – Royal Scots Regimental Museum

Traigh Allt Chailgeag looking east   © Copyright Ian

Morrison and licensed for reuse under this Creative Commons Licence.

ABOUT THE AUTHOR

Charlie Parkes

My brain and I have been together for over 70 years achieving some remarkable things and some dismal failures! Measure once - cut once – buy another worktop, for example! These days I do find it harder to deal with irrelevant data. All I need is the bottom line. If I want more data, I will ask for it or Google it, or just switch off from my loved ones. I can be forgetful and find it hard to recall things but that is normal and does not mean that I am losing my marbles. Indeed, I have a full tin on my bookshelf.

I know that my brain has filed huge amounts of data unconsciously and it just takes a bit longer tracking it down. It is all in there somewhere! However, it is difficult to find what you do not know the brain has stored for a rainy day and there is no index or search engine! Suddenly, something pops into my consciousness and I wonder, "Where did that come from? What triggered that thought? And why?" As founder of Swanwick Men's Shed, I have observed various forms of Alzheimer's and dementia at close hand and fear the onset of these debilitating conditions in my old age. It is terribly sad to see skilled woodworkers unable to recognise the tools and machinery they once used to create masterpieces in wood. I have also seen how people have regained the ability to enjoy life as a member of the shed. For some it has been a lifesaver. For a bereaved member the shed becomes their family.

To offset dementia I keep The Times General Knowledge crossword books dotted round the house to dip in to, as and when. It is a comfort to find that my brain function improves with practice but I also find them rather soporific.

I also find that instinctively shooting clay pigeons on a fast and furious drive proves that my brain, eye and body can still coordinate. My motto is "Still shooting. Still writing. Still living."

Over many years, I have written books on countryside law and conservation. Getting every comma and full stop correct in a legal text is pretty tedious and tiresome stuff. In 1996, I wrote a small book of Shaggy Dog Stories that was purely fictional and imaginative and great fun to do. I relished the freedom to write without constriction. The title and some of the tales hark back to stories told by my father from his army days, and I enjoyed embellishing them with detail based upon characters I developed from friends and family. I truly enjoy visualising a location or a character and describing them with a picture in words. Imagination gives you the freedom to create your own characters and personalities. They are the actors in your theatre bringing your words, actions and locations to life to entertain an audience. In your imagination, you can do anything thought to be impossible.

The story line can take over all my waking thoughts and I jot down notes, wherever I am, and rush home to type them up. Never let an idea get away as you may not find it again. Imagination can take you wherever you want in the world at any time in history, or the future, even to places that do not exist. I find the mental process invigorating and exciting and realise that the old brain is not dead or dying! Being creative has been a hugely enjoyable, fun and rewarding experience leaving the brain energised as if it was on fire.

Creative writing is a great exercise for the brain - all you need is a spark. As Jane Austen said, "Indulge your imagination in every possible flight." [Pride and Prejudice.] You do not need to publish just try short stories or your life story. No need for them to be fiction either, just write about what you know or have done.

In 2015, I took my wife on a railway holiday on the West Highland Line and Hogwarts Express. On the bleak and rain swept misty Rannoch Moor I saw a young woman leave the train and disappear into the mist. I began to imagine what might befall her alone in the boggy wilderness. I told my "sister" Carla and fifteen years later found a spark of an idea that fired the imagination for a romantic mystery novel about The Hidden Glen in the Scottish Highlands, published in her name on Amazon as an EBook and paperback.

Rudyard Kipling, the author, not the cake-maker said, "I keep six honest serving-men (They taught me all I knew); their names are What and Why and When and How and Where and Who. Choose a person, a location or situation, apply the 5Ws and you are up and running. The data is all in that brain of yours somewhere.

BOOKS BY THIS AUTHOR

Shaggy Dog Stories Tales Of The Countryside

I published Shaggy Dog Stories in 1996 selling over 10,000 copies. With only two copies left on my shelf, I decided it was time to republish and search my brain for some new material. I found one hundred percent more new stories and published on Amazon in 2023. The new edition consists of thirty-two stories illustrated with line drawings and featuring Spot the beer-drinking, domino-playing shaggy dog who pops up throughout the book to prove that man is a dog's best friend!

The Hidden Glen

It's Fresher's Week at Portsmouth University and Emma is thrown into the melting pot that independent life and university bring. She befriends three girls from different backgrounds and levels in society. Perhaps these innocents abroad were attracted to each other by their common denominator – being insular, not worldly wise, not streetwise. but together they would look to each other and after each other in a lasting friendship. Explore Emma's childhood, her "Uni" friends, the men in her life, her sailing and rambling adventures from Scotland to the south coast, France, Italy and the Peak District. Through difficult, emotional times, she is guided by the wisdom of her wonderfully philosophical "Nannee Jane" who always finds positive outcomes on her encounters. rathe like Jane Austen. Is there a link between Nannee Jane a Jane Austen apart from family connections with Chawt

Following several false starts and one disturbing end to a relationship, Emma continues her quest to find her perfect man. Hoping for peace and solitude away from nine-to-five in a London fashion house, she embarks on a lone, wild-walking, trek in the Scottish highlands where she meets a mysterious fellow traveller in a remote fishing hut. The events that follow in the Hidden Glen remain unfathomable, magical, mystical and beyond all human reasoning.

Emma returns to her family and university friends where she reveals almost all her secrets. Several years later Emma retraces her steps, but this time she is not alone, in a quest to find the man, love and the happiness she left behind in the Hidden Glen. Discover whether she unravels the mysteries of the glen and if there is a potential return to reality for the lovers. Illuminated with Jane Austen quotations about love, marriage and happiness as relevant now as the day she wrote them. Lavishly illustrated with photographs so you can walk in Emma's footsteps or even visit all the locations except, that is, for the Hidden Glen.

Boy From The Building Site

The idea came from Neale, a kitchen fitter replacing defective doors and panels. He did an excellent job not stopping for a drink or a chat and was done and dust free in three days. Most fortunately, I managed to have a brief chat starting with the usual opening gambit, "Are you local?" Yes, he is local now having been in the area for many years but he said, "My dad was a Scouser and I lived on a building site for six years before oving down here." Neale triggered my imagination about the and adventures of a boy living in a cabin. The timescale of 70s fitted my own very different childhood but as writing sed, I found the brain was working overtime dragging from my life experiences and locations to illustrate the t is a nostalgic bit of fun, total fiction but containing rents and people from my past.

Printed in Great Britain
by Amazon